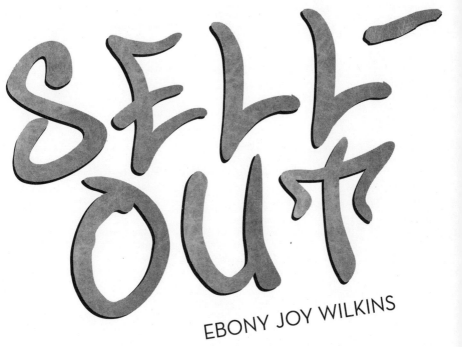

SELL-OUT

EBONY JOY WILKINS

SCHOLASTIC PRESS / NEW YORK

Copyright © 2010 by Ebony Joy Wilkins

Library of Congress Cataloging-in-Publication Data
Wilkins, Ebony Joy.
Sellout / by Ebony Joy Wilkins. — 1st ed.
p. cm.
Summary: NaTasha loves her life of affluence in Adams Park, but her grandmother
fears she has lost touch with her roots and whisks her off to Harlem, where NaTasha
meets rough, streetwise girls at a crisis center and finds the courage to hold her
own against them.
[1. Self-realization — Fiction. 2. African Americans — Fiction. 3. Social classes —
Fiction. 4. Identity — Fiction. 5. Grandmothers — Fiction. 6. Ballet — Fiction.
7. New York (N.Y.) — Fiction.] I. Title.
PZ7.W64853Sel 2010
[Fic] — dc22
2009020522

ISBN 978-0-545-10928-4

10 9 8 7 6 5 4 3 2 1   10 11 12 13 14

Printed in the U.S.A.   23
First edition, July 2010

The text was set in 13 pt. Perpetua. The display type is Street Soul.
Book design by Lillie Howard

TO MY FAMILY

I PULLED UP on the front of my pink leotard and turned to the mirror to look at my large backside. No change there. I stretched the fabric tightly across my chest and frowned. Almost a sophomore and still no need for a bra. So much for cutting all those carbs. The calories would always hit us black girls in all the wrong places.

I might as well eat the carbs; *they* made me happy.

I stared into the mirror, letting reality set in. I had curves. I would always have curves. My leotard rode up in the back, piercing the fat in my butt cheeks. But I was used to that.

I was different from the other dancers, who were all white and thin as rails. I was dark skinned and "big boned," but the girls never cared. They were my friends.

I would never look like them, but my leotard was freshly ironed, my stockings were bleached to perfection and smelled like an ice cream sundae on a hot summer day, and there wasn't a lick of ash on my skin anywhere.

I arched my shoulders back and stood tall. My mom always told me that if my clothes looked nice, then my day would go exactly how I wanted it to. According to the Miriam Jennings School of First Impressions, my ballet recital tonight would go just fine.

I called Mom into my room for the inspection.

"You look great, Tash," she said, standing behind me in the mirror. She tugged down on the leotard, trying to cover my exposed cheeks. She waved her hands for me to turn this way and that. "Is this the new one you girls bought last weekend?"

I nodded. Her approval was crucial. One mishap and I would be in front of the mirror an extra hour. I modeled like a doll on display while she examined me from head to toe. She even stood on her tiptoes to look at my hair. Her face twisted into a frown.

"Well, you almost look ready to dance your first ballet recital," she said, "but let's get started on that head. We don't want to go and scare off all the attention you're going to get, now do we?"

Every time I sat in front of my mother to get my hair done, I felt like I was risking my life. The hot iron would dangle dangerously close to my skin while she was lost in conversation about fashion, forgetting all about my hair.

Tonight, as she greased my scalp and leaned her stomach in against my back, she talked about the new collection of earrings she saw at the mall and our neighbor's bag that she had to have.

"I have to know where she got that bag. You think Macy's or Saks?" she asked.

I ignored her and focused on dodging the iron to avoid serious burn marks.

My mom separated my hair into sections and added a drop of styling lotion to each piece. She steadied my head with one hand and pulled the hot curling iron through my hair with the other. The hair fell softly away from the iron.

I retraced her steps with my hand. It wasn't long ago that my mom and I would sit for hours while she twisted my hair into a labyrinth of braids, decorating the ends with multi-colored beads. Then after elementary school, I stopped wearing my hair in braids. My friends and I started wearing our hair down but it took more effort to make my hair flow like the other girls'.

"Mom, I'm sure you'll be able to find the bag," I told her, faking interest in the mystery of the bag's location. The iron swung toward my ear and I ducked out of the way. My mother didn't seem to notice.

"I don't know, Tash," she said, pulling the iron away from my face. "Maybe you can look it up online for me. Or I could go over and ask Marlene if I can borrow some sugar and then peek around to see if I can get a better look."

I couldn't believe she would risk getting caught, all for a bag.

"Mom, why don't you just ask her?"

She looked at me like I had just taken the holy name of Gucci in vain. But it was worth risking her death stare to get her to stop going on about that bag. Talking fashion just meant I would be stuck in front of her with my wild hair that much longer.

"I don't need to," she said, tugging harder on my head. "When you head to the city with Tilly this weekend, you're going to check for me."

Tilly was my grandmother. We didn't shop when we were together. We hung out and talked. I looked forward to her visits like most kids looked forward to summer break. When school ended, Tilly came for a weekend and took me back to Harlem with her.

That had been our routine for as long as I could remember. With the school year behind me, Tilly and I could relax and enjoy each other's company. Less pressure and less worrying when Tilly was around. I certainly wasn't going to waste our time with a pocketbook scavenger hunt all over Manhattan.

"What time is Tilly getting in anyway?" I asked her, changing the subject.

"Your father went to the station almost an hour ago," she said, glancing at her watch while she pulled the iron through another section of my hair. "They will meet us at the dance center."

Tilly wasn't a fan of our preppy small town. *Too many white folks and not enough jerk chicken.* That's what she told people when they asked about her visits to New Jersey.

Everyone here loved Tilly, but she was fine to stay in her apartment in the city and let us come to her. She only made the hour-long trek on the bus when I had something important, like tonight's recital, going on at school.

"I hope no one tried to crowd her seat this time," I said. My mom laughed at the thought. I pulled away from her grip slightly, the thought of Tilly sitting in the audience suddenly making me anxious. I closed my eyes and forced my brain to rehearse the choreography I'd been practicing for two months.

Practice did not make perfect in my case. I always *looked* good, but I was as graceful as an elephant on ice skates. *A black ballet dancer?* Tilly had thought it was ridiculous. But my friends had sworn to disown me if I didn't at least audition. Leotards and pointe shoes — just one more way I stood out like a sore thumb.

Sometimes I wished Marcia would have changed her mind about me. She ran a tight ship and could have kicked me out of the troupe so I could have gone back to volleyball. Thank God tonight was the last night. I think even my parents were tired of seeing me trip across the stage, no matter how good I looked faking it.

"Your hair has grown since last month," my mother said. She pulled on the longest of my dark brown strands. My friends and I had a contest going to see who could grow their hair the longest by the end of the school year. Heather was in the lead. She could wrap one arm behind her back and almost touch the tip of her soft strands. I got a straightening perm every two months, but with my natural hair, no matter how many strokes I brushed at night, I didn't have any chance of winning. I might as well have been sporting an Afro.

Sometimes I dreamed about my hair flowing down my back the way Heather's did. Not likely. It wouldn't look right anyway. Long silky hair would clash with my dark chocolate skin, curvy hips, big lips, and wide nose.

I went back to my choreography.

"Yeah, but not long enough," I said. My mother pulled my hair so hard I had to look up at her.

"Remember we talked about not comparing ourselves to others?" she asked. Her large brown eyes were round with concern. Of course I remembered. We talked about it all the time. It was a little easier said than done, though. I hadn't seen someone who looked like me, other than her, in awhile.

"Then you won't need me to search high and low for that new bag after all, just so you can *fit in*?" I asked. I waited for her to lash out at me. Instead, she pulled my hair with mock force and went back to my hair without saying a word. I reached for the pink ballet ribbon all the girls wore in their hair for recitals and weaved it in and out of my fingers. I needed to tie it into my hair somehow.

The other dancers would gather their hair into a bun and lace the pink ribbon around the outside. Uniform. That was how Marcia wanted our appearance to be. In ballet, that was how it was supposed to be.

My mom reached down and took the ribbon from me. She lost her grip on the iron and it crashed into the sink bowl along with the ribbon. I jutted out of the way just in time.

"NaTasha, are you okay?" she said, kissing my cheek.

I leaned over the sink to see if I still had a pink ribbon to wear for the recital. Luckily the ribbon was untouched. We jumped as Heather bounded through the door.

"You're just in time, Heather," my mom said. "I'm finishing up NaTasha's hair and trying not to leave any permanent scars."

My best friend laughed and squeezed past us to sit on top of the closed toilet seat lid.

"Today's performance is going to be the best yet," she squealed. "I can feel it." Heather had feelings about everything— a rainstorm three states away, a secret clearance sale at Macy's, or an unannounced pop quiz in Algebra. No matter what the occasion, she could feel it coming.

Mom and I looked at each other. She winked at me and dried the ends of the iron with a hand towel before handling it again.

"So, why is it that today is going to be the best yet?" I asked, egging Heather on even though I knew once she got going, it would be hard to stop her.

"This recital marks the end of our freshman year," she said. "Now we can spend the entire summer practicing chore-ography, shopping for new clothes, and talking about the guys. I already got invitations to a few parties, and of course, you have to come with me, although Melissa's can only hap-pen if she doesn't go to France for the summer, but whatever. We'll party and shop and dance. Won't it be great?"

Heather was practically bouncing up and down. She should be the one shopping for my mother's fancy bags, not me. I rolled my eyes at her.

"Calm down, crazy," I laughed. "Let's just try to get through tonight first."

She stuck her tongue out at me when my mom looked away.

Mom curled the last section of hair. I pulled a few flyaway pieces from my face and held the ribbon out to her.

"You *really* need help with the ribbon?" she asked, looking from me to Heather.

"Nope, we can handle that part, thanks," Heather told her, jumping up. My mom waved and left us alone. Heather ran her fingers through my hair. "This summer really is going to be so great."

We said the same thing every year. And every year by the end of July we were itching to get back to school already.

"The best yet, I can just feel it," I said, mocking her.

Heather flipped me the bird, then held out her hand for the ribbon. With the exception of my rounder hips, shorter hair, and darker skin, we looked like twins in our pink short-sleeved leotards and pink tutus. I handed her the ribbon, laughing. Reaching behind me, she pulled the hair away from my face and tied the ribbon ends into a bow.

Heather frowned. "Oh my God, I almost forgot!" she shrieked, running over to her pocketbook.

"What?" I asked, fiddling to get my ribbon just right. It looked like a headband.

"I brought you something," she said, pulling two thin brown scarves from her bag.

"What are those for?" I asked, even though I already had a feeling I knew where she was headed. "Heather, you know Marcia will flip if my ribbon doesn't look like every-one else's."

"Don't worry, just turn around for a minute."

She untied my pink ribbon and reached for a comb.

"I don't think so." I raised my hand to stop her.

"Trust me, Tash," she said, moving my hand away, "I won't ruin what Miriam did."

I thought about all the trouble we had gotten into over the years. Our sneak trips to the mall, running away from home once for three hours, and stealing gum balls from Mr. Tomkins at the grocery on the corner—all Heather's bright ideas.

She tilted her head and smiled at me innocently. I folded my arms across my chest and raised an eyebrow.

"Seriously, Tash," she said. "You'll look great, just like the rest of us."

"Fine, but if this doesn't work," I warned her, "you'll have to answer to my mother on your own. And hurry up so we're not late."

I turned around so she could get to work. Heather couldn't mess this up. I couldn't mess this up. I could feel Heather pulling my hair while weaving a fake bun into the back of my head.

"Problem solved," Heather said proudly. She turned me toward the mirror. "Check it out."

I turned around and looked at the bun of scarves at the back of my head. It wasn't perfect, but it did the trick. I thought of Tilly and my stomach spun. I pushed the feeling aside. It had to be okay to fit in just this once.

CHAPTER TWO

WE PULLED UP to the Adams Park Dance Center and my insides were dancing before we even found a parking spot. The idea of making any mistakes onstage tonight had my stomach in a maze of knots.

Before volleyball games I felt excited and couldn't wait to get out on the court. Hours before a match, I'd picture myself leaping to set balls and slamming them over the net past my opponents. I was great out on the court, but ballet was a whole different story. I wasn't a star in my leotard and tutu.

Ballet wasn't for me, and Tilly was the only one who really understood. My parents said it would be good for me to try something new. Heather said it would make us more popular. Not true. I still had the same friends now as I had at the beginning of the year.

After we parked I sat there frozen in my seat. Heather stood with one door open, bribing me to exit. I spotted Tilly and Dad waiting at the entrance—too late to run back home and hide. I slammed the door behind me and put on a smile.

"Hey, girl, get over here and give your Tilly a hug," Tilly yelled across the lot when she saw me. She waved a bright red hat that matched her loud, red-and-black pantsuit. When Tilly was invited to an event, she dressed the part. To her, if it required an invitation, it required a new outfit. My first ballet recital tonight was no exception, even though she wasn't convinced I should be involved at all. *Why are you going to give up something you love, to dance around with those silly white girls?*

"Hey, Tilly," I said, thinking back to our talks about quitting volleyball. "You ready for this?"

"Of course I'm ready, baby," she said, squeezing me tight. It was good to have her arms wrapped around me. Her tight embrace felt like glue holding me together in one piece. I was afraid that when she let go, I might fall apart right in front of her. "Now, you make me proud up there, you hear?"

"You got it," I said. But I wasn't feeling quite as sure as I sounded.

Heather and I joined the other dancers for our warm-up routine. I stretched both hands over my head and pulled down gently. Moving on to the next stretch on my own, I forgot the rest of the group and pushed my nose and body as close to the floor as I could. I couldn't stop thinking about my hair.

"NaTasha, this is exactly the kind of break in formation we do not need during crunch time," Marcia barked. She was meant to be an instructor . . . of anything. She just liked telling anyone who would listen what they should and should not be doing. "If we're together during stretches, we'll be together onstage. Wait for the group, please."

I rolled my eyes underneath closed lids. From day one she'd been extra hard on me. She was right that I needed to stay focused, but I couldn't help myself. My mind kept wandering out beyond the maroon stage curtain.

What would Tilly think? Had I practiced enough? Was Matt Billings in the audience? He was hands down the cutest guy in our class. What he would be doing at a ballet recital was beyond me, but I thought about him watching me anyway.

I peeked at the other dancers, who all had their legs outstretched and noses to the floor. We'd practiced our routines for two months, and I knew every step as well as the others. The show would go smoothly now if only my body would cooperate. I told myself there was nothing to worry about.

Marcia walked us back to a small, mirrored room off to stage left. The girls whispered excitedly to one another about who had come to watch them. Heather went on and on about something, but I couldn't even respond. Instead, I snuck a look through the heavy curtain. I found my family sitting in one of the orchestra sections toward the center of the auditorium.

Tilly looked smothered, like someone heavy was sitting on her lap. She was on the aisle seat in the fourth row, hugging her pocketbook tightly to her chest.

Once, Tilly and I had made fun of ballet dancers on television, saying they looked like flamingos. Now I was one of them. I would have to make this up to her somehow.

Only five minutes until showtime. All the seats were filled.

"Okay, folks, this is it," Marcia whispered. I dropped the curtain and grabbed Heather's arm. Marcia had us hold hands in a circle. She didn't strike me as the praying type, but she bowed her head and so did we. "Let's make this a great show. Remember your spacing and formations, but most important, have a good time."

We pumped our hands down together at the same time and whispered "dance" like we were vying for a championship trophy.

"Hey, Tash, I just *love* the hair." Stephanie Bonner stood with her hands on her hips and smirked at her dance groupie peons. "You finally got the look right. Marcia must be thrilled."

Stephanie was the best dancer at Adams Park. She was blond, tiny, perfect, and popular, and she knew how good she was. I felt sick, like she had punched me in the chest. Somehow after a full year of her insults, I still didn't know how to respond when she lashed out at me.

"It does look great, doesn't it, Bones?" Heather stepped in between Stephanie and me like a Secret Service agent and wrapped an arm protectively around my shoulders. "It almost looks better than yours. Hey, break a leg out there tonight, would you?"

Stephanie looked like she'd been bitch slapped. No one ever talked to her that way. She narrowed her eyes at us and stalked off with a small group of ballerinas stumbling along behind her. Heather giggled and hugged me tight.

When she pulled away her arm bumped the scarves. I could feel something hanging and motioned frantically for her to fix it. She fiddled with something quickly before we scooted into our places onstage, ten in the front row and ten in the back. "You know one day she'll come after you," I whispered.

"Whatever, I'm not scared of her," Heather said, raising her arms and settling into position. She balanced perfectly on one pointed toe. "She just likes to bully people. You know she's harmless."

Stephanie had single-handedly alienated an entire grade after starting some rumor about the boys not wearing deodorant. I definitely didn't want to be on her bad side.

"Okay, but don't say I didn't warn you. . . . Thanks for sticking up for me," I said.

"You know it, girl," Heather said. She smiled brightly. I didn't know what I'd ever do without my best friend at my side.

The music started playing. It sounded the same as it had during practices, but now with the curtain seconds away from opening, it seemed different. My head was spinning but I hadn't even started moving yet. A wave of nausea sped through my system, like I'd just had milk that should have been tossed the week before. The curtain started to open and I held my breath.

I could see Tilly looking around for me, her purse still held tightly to her chest. The curtain lifted all the way. We were on.

Hundreds of eyes stared at us, waiting for us to move. We listened for our cue. The music echoed off the walls in surround sound. People lined the walls of the auditorium. Not one seat was open, standing room only. I chose a spot on the far wall across from the stage to focus on and help my turning, just like in practice.

"I'm going to throw up," I whispered to Heather.

"Me too," she mouthed back.

I closed my eyes and hummed along with the first five bars of Tchaikovsky's *Swan Lake*. On the sixth bar, when the bell part began, we moved our toes from first position to third and back again. We lifted our arms in half circles and spun like dolls, puppets attached to strings.

I kept in time with the music when the drums began to pound. I stretched my body harder than in practice and poured everything I had into our first pirouette turns. I bent my body in two and swept my arms across the floor just like we practiced. Marcia would be so proud.

We glided across the stage, flitting like little butterflies. After lowering gracefully to touch our toes, we lifted again, and tiptoed slowly into one large circle in the center of the stage. Our bodies leaned into the circle and out again, creating a sort of ocean wave.

Marcia was a huge fan of kicking lines, adding them into almost every routine. We first kicked at waist level to show off our flexibility. Stephanie glared at me from her position, gloating over her perfect form. I kicked higher, but couldn't wait to break away to the next pose.

Pure adrenaline took over toward the last movement. My legs shook as I traveled across the stage. My head began to spin out of control, like my brain was in a washing machine set on high. My turning spot on the wall was now lost to me.

The other dancers locked arms with me. The beat sped up during the last series of eight counts of the song and so did my heartbeat. It felt like we were descending from the highest roller coaster in the world. I wanted to lift my arms and scream as loud as I could.

The music accelerated and we began our double turns. I smiled and looked to find Tilly. I landed my turn, but Tilly wasn't watching. Instead, she was searching through her purse. Maybe her cell was ringing.

Our leaps were next and I was already dizzy from the turns. I brushed away a few hairs that were blowing in my face and took a deep breath. I could feel the scarves weighing heavier in my hair, but I kept jumping, arms level, legs outstretched.

Dad was on the edge of his chair, swaying along to the music. My mother and Tilly looked like they were watching a completely different show, their eyes wide open, almost in shock. The dancers leaped into the final formation.

One at a time we sashayed off the stage. It wasn't until my turn to exit that I realized the scarves weren't in my hair anymore. They had slipped and were now draped around my shoulders.

I searched for Marcia in the wings. Her eyes were stuck on me, and not because of my perfect leaps, either. One break from formation and she would flip, scarves or no scarves. Grabbing the scarves was out of the question.

I prayed Matt Billings couldn't see me now.

The room spun like I was on a broken carnival ride still in motion. I could hear a gasp from the direction of the crowd, no doubt intended for me.

I wanted lightning to strike me right at that moment. At least I would stop spinning. Now *that* would be a good show. Sweat beads prickled every part of my body, including my ears. My heartbeat banged more loudly than the music. I couldn't hear a thing anymore.

I wasn't sure in which direction I was turning, but finally I was offstage. I bent down toward my knees so my vision could clear, and peeked out at the remaining dancers onstage. They each detoured around our exiting point, not like we had practiced at all.

I looked around the stage. My scarves lay right in the path of our dramatic exit.

Two more dancers needed to make it beyond the scarves and through the curtain, Heather and Stephanie. The scarves were too far out onstage for me to grab them. I could see Marcia glaring. I tried to swallow but my throat felt like it was slowly closing up.

I motioned at my hair and waved frantically for Heather to stop spinning. But she couldn't see me.

Luckily, Heather's turn was off balance so she missed the scarves by a few inches. I thought we were in the clear until Stephanie completed the perfect twirl right on top of the scarves, like a dreidel. She slipped and fell hard.

A hush fell over the crowd. Stephanie was sprawled out on the stage, holding the scarves in one hand and her ankle in the other. The curtain closed swiftly without any applause from the audience, just the sound of hushed whispering.

I ran to Stephanie along with the others as quickly as I could. "Stephanie, I'm so sorry. Are you okay?" I wanted to patch her back together and rewind time to undo the mess.

"You should be sorry," Stephanie yelled through her tears. Everyone, including Marcia, turned to look at me. I wondered if the audience could hear what was going on. Tilly had probably left the building by this point. I hovered over Stephanie, not knowing what else to do or say.

One of the dancers bent down to inspect Stephanie's ankle. I bent down, too. Stephanie leaned in toward me, so her face was just inches from my own.

"What did you think? That no one would notice your *fake bun?*" She mouthed it roughly, like the words were fighting to stay inside her mouth. "You're more stupid than I thought, NaTasha *Jennings*," she said before throwing the scarves at my feet.

Marcia and a few of the girls gently moved Stephanie off-stage and waved around frantically for the curtain call. One of Stephanie's peons ran to get her parents.

I was pretty sure no one in the audience wanted to see me back up there, not even my own family. So, when the curtain went up and Heather reached for my hand, I shook her off and ran backstage. I left the scarves right there on the stage floor.

CHAPTER THREE

I BEAT MY family out to the car. When they finally caught up to me, my heart was still racing as if I had never left the stage. As far as I was concerned, I was never going back onstage again.

No one said a word. Tilly and my parents quickly strapped themselves in and my dad couldn't have started the engine fast enough. I wanted to bury my head deep in a sandpit somewhere far from home. I was relieved that I was going to be leaving town for a while. In Tilly's neighborhood I could hide, take a deep breath, and relax again. No one there would know what happened tonight. I certainly wouldn't be the one to bring it up. I wasn't so sure about Tilly, though.

Other families were starting to trickle out of the building as we drove out of the parking lot. I slid far down in my seat to avoid making any eye contact. I turned toward Tilly in the seat next to me and searched her face for a sign as to what she was thinking. She shook her head back and forth.

"Something like this happened to me a long time ago," Tilly said. I was glad she finally broke the ice. I raised my eyebrows and waited. When I could tell we'd pulled out onto Main Street, I pulled myself back into a seated position. "I, too, was trying to be someone I wasn't and got caught."

The story that followed was a familiar one. Tilly used to nanny for a white family. She was invited to a party in their home as a guest and as the story goes, she got *too* comfortable. "Some of the other guests assumed I was the hired help and decided I should clean up after them instead of *join* them for dinner."

Tilly had gotten mad when the other guests treated her like a servant.

"How'd you get over the humiliation?" I asked. My dad glanced at me in his rearview mirror.

"I ran and hid for a while," Tilly said, "but I came back to face them again when I was able to, just like you'll have to one day."

The idea of facing Stephanie and Marcia made me nauseous. Good thing we were pulling into our driveway, because everything in my stomach felt like it was about to come out. As soon as we were parked, I ran in to the restroom, while my parents and Tilly rested in the living room. I could hear them talking about me through the bathroom door.

"I told you not to expose her to all of this," Tilly said. "This could have all been avoided. Why do you think I warned you both about living here?"

"Everything is fine, Tilly," Dad told her. "The girls danced a great show and Stephanie's fall didn't appear to be serious. This will pass and practice at the dance center will go back to normal in no time at all."

Wearing the scarves couldn't possibly be that big of a deal. All the hottest fashion magazines had models wearing them. I bet even my mother had plans to add a few to her own wardrobe. Besides, with a bun, I looked like all the other dancers. Marcia wanted uniformity, so I gave it to her. Really, it was all *her* fault Stephanie fell.

The grandfather clock tolled nine o'clock and jolted me back to life. I tiptoed out of the bathroom and sat just outside the living room so I couldn't be seen.

"Walter Jennings, this is bigger than that dance center and you know it," Tilly said. She never used my dad's full name. Or anyone's for that matter, unless she meant business. Her voice was louder than it had been earlier. I could tell she was getting angry.

I focused on the three-piece art display of African dancers hanging on the wall across from me. Those dancers had all kinds of scarves tied in their hair and on their bodies. What was so wrong with how I wore mine?

"Tilly, this is normal behavior for teenagers," my dad added. "Every week they are fighting with someone new."

"He's right about that, Tilly," my mom said. "Then a week later everyone is friends again. We shouldn't blow this too far out of proportion."

"Girl, this town ain't normal," Tilly shot back. "There ain't nothing normal about her being the only person of color in an entire school district. Nothing normal at all."

When Tilly got angry, it was "girl" this and "girl" that.

"So, Tilly, what are you suggesting we do about this situation?" Dad said. My dad was the practical one in the family. If there was a problem, he didn't want to talk circles around it, he wanted a solution. Tilly and Mom weren't ready to end it that quickly.

"She needs to be around our own people for once," Tilly said. "She's been here her whole life. She needs to know who she is and where she comes from. I need her to know these things and, right now, she has no idea."

"So, tell her what you want her to know, Tilly," my dad said, challenging her. "You keep talking about what NaTasha needs, but I think I know my own daughter and NaTasha knows exactly who she is. . . ."

"Your daughter wore some scarves to cover up the beautiful, kinky black hair the good Lord gave her, and you think there is no problem?" Tilly interrupted. "It's bad enough you use some iron to straighten out the kinks in her hair that weren't ever meant to be straight at all. It's no wonder the child is confused. I'd be confused, too."

My mom didn't say anything. I wanted to peek around the corner and see the expressions on their faces so bad. It must have looked like they were watching a bloody horror film and the main character just got stabbed.

"Look, we're on the same side here," my dad said in his "make peace" voice. "We all want to protect Tash, but let's remember that bad stuff in her life will come in all colors."

"But keeping her isolated here in this town isn't helping her," Tilly said. "There isn't anything we can just *tell* her; she has to go out into the world and experience things for herself, good and bad. What she needs is a few weeks working with me and the girls at the center. She's old enough to do that now."

For as long as I could remember, Tilly had volunteered at Amber's Place, a safe place for girls in the city.

There was a long pause. Surely, my parents wouldn't go for a long stay in the city.

"Well, Tilly, that would give NaTasha the kind of chance you're talking about." my dad finished. "It's NaTasha's decision, of course."

A few weeks?

There was a space next to Tilly on the sofa. I eased into the room, trying not to draw any attention. My foot caught the piano bench instead, and it crashed loudly onto the hardwood floor.

All three of them snapped their heads in my direction. No one moved a muscle. It was like I was some science experiment they'd mixed together and were now waiting for the reaction.

Tilly looked tense and tired, but she smiled. I glanced at her hands. Whenever she wasn't talking, her hands spoke for her. Tilly had her fists squeezed so tight, her knuckles were white, like she'd been making biscuits and rubbing her hands in grease and flour.

"Tilly, was it really that bad?" I whispered. Tilly nodded and walked past me to the stairs. I'd never stayed with Tilly longer than one week. But now things were different. Spending the entire summer in Adams Park was out of the question. Maybe a few extra weeks away *would* help to make everything okay again.

*   *   *

All night I dreamed of tripping Stephanie with my scarves. I woke up covered in sweat and more embarrassed than I had been after the recital.

The doorbell rang early and I already knew who was at the door. I wasn't in the mood for any company, but there was no way Heather was going to leave without seeing me. As soon as I opened the front door, she grabbed me by the elbow and marched me up to my room.

"What the hell happened last night?" she asked, collapsing onto my bed.

I wanted to leave the whole recital incident behind me. But Heather's eyes were glued to me, and I knew that wasn't an option. Her expression was harsh, like I'd personally offended her.

"I don't know what happened," I told her. "You know as much as I do."

"Were you messing with the scarves?" she asked. I didn't like having my best friend sound like a judge or having to defend myself. I glared at her.

"When would I have had the time?" I asked her. "In between double turns?"

"Well, scarves don't just jump out of hair all on their own," she said.

"You're the one who gave them to me in the first place," I reminded her. She sat up quickly, like I had threatened to expose her dirty little secret.

"I tied them as tight as they would go and you know it," she said. She folded her arms across her chest and sighed. We sat in silence for a few minutes. No need to argue about the scarves. The damage was already done and there was no turning back.

"You think Stephanie will ever forgive me?" I asked, already knowing the answer. Heather shrugged, but remained quiet. "Well, good thing I'm leaving town then."

I pulled my black-and-white carry-on luggage bag out of the closet and opened one of my dresser drawers.

"What am I supposed to do for a whole week at the start of summer when we are supposed to be doing everything together?" Heather said. "Oh my God, it feels like you're leaving forever."

"It isn't forever, Heather, it is only a week tops," I lied. No way could I tell her I might extend my stay. "And you know I leave at the same time every year."

"A week *is* forever, though," she said.

I started to unzip my bag, but Heather stopped me, falling across it and clutching her heart with one hand and her forehead with the other. She was the definition of *drama queen*. She could sniffle and make her teacher send her to the nurse's office. If her parents' car got nicked in the parking lot at the mall, in Heather's version of the story, they had a near-death experience.

"Who am I going to shop with?" she asked. "Who am I going to eat with? Who am I going to talk about the guys with?"

Since I could remember, Heather and I were attached at the hip. Spending a few weeks apart and only being able to talk on the phone would be hard.

"They do have phones in Harlem," I reminded her. "I'll call you every night and the time will fly by. And I'll e-mail you. I'll be back before you know it."

She waved her hand like she wasn't trying to hear anything I had to say.

"You're going to forget all about me, I just know it," she said. "When you get back, you're going to be a completely different person. I bet I won't even be able to recognize you."

"Oh, please, give me a break," I replied.

"I guess we'll just have to see," she said, folding her arms across her chest. "I really don't understand why you have to go for so long."

When I was younger, my visits with Tilly didn't extend beyond a weekend. The past few years, I started staying a little longer, though the first extended weekend, I was so homesick my parents drove up to get me before my planned stay had ended. It was different now. I was sure I was ready to stay a few weeks and leave the drama behind and start fresh.

I pulled out whatever clothes were clean and started throwing them in my luggage. I threw a T-shirt to Heather and nodded toward my suitcase. Since I would probably be helping Tilly at her volunteer job, I needed something.a little dressier than jeans and T-shirts. I grabbed a new white tank top and a red skirt Heather and I had bought at the mall a few weeks ago.

"This is such a bad idea," Heather said, throwing in more shirts. "And why do you need so many clothes for one week anyway?"

Of course it was a bad idea to Heather; her best friend was deserting her for what she thought was one week. I felt bad for not telling her the truth about what I was considering. No way would she take the news well. That I knew for sure.

With Tilly acting so disappointed and determined to show me my roots, my extended stay might even be a bad idea for me, too. But staying to face my problem with the two ballet Nazis was out of the question.

Tilly's life in Harlem wasn't glamorous — too many people in too small of a space where everyone knew everyone's business. But even overcrowded Harlem was sounding better than home.

"It's just another visit with Tilly, Heather," I said.

I had a hard time believing this myself, though. I knew Tilly wouldn't take the incident last night lightly. But, seriously, I wore *scarves* in my hair. I hadn't tried to skip school or kill anyone. I wore a silly hairstyle. If Stephanie hadn't slipped on my scarves, I bet no one would have even noticed they were in my hair at all. Surely, the time away would fly by and I'd return to my normal life.

Packing was overrated. I shut my dresser drawers and picked up my clean clothes hamper and dumped it inside the suitcase.

"There, packing all done," I said. I flopped down next to Heather on the bed.

"Remember when we stuck those up there?" she asked, nodding toward the one hundred glow-in-the-dark stars on my ceiling. She took a deep breath and let it out slowly.

"Of course I remember, I almost broke my neck standing on my desk trying to stick them up there," I said. We both laughed.

"Let's make another wish," she said. We'd been doing this for years. Usually we wished for boys to talk to us. Heather grabbed my hand and we closed our eyes. My wish was that Stephanie wouldn't still be mad at me by the time I got back from Tilly's place.

My leotard and tutu were in a pile on the floor. We both saw them at the same time. Heather picked them up and tossed both into my bag.

"Just in case you want to practice while you're gone," she said. I smiled, but pulled the leotard and tutu back out and tossed them onto the floor.

"Actually, Heather, I doubt I'll be needing these ever again," I said. No harm in starting fresh right away.

Heather took a deep breath. "What are you talking about? Is this because of what happened at the show?"

I shook my head no, but she didn't notice. She was too busy getting herself all worked up.

"Because if it is, Tash, you know how kids are around here," she said. "They'll tease you for a while and forget all about it in no time."

Yeah, I did know kids around here. They were my friends, but it still hurt to be the brunt of their jokes all the time.

"Yeah, I know," I answered her.

"Really, Stephanie isn't even that mad," Heather said.

I wondered how Heather knew exactly how Stephanie was feeling, especially because we didn't ever talk to her outside of ballet, under any circumstances. Heather noticed the shocked look on my face.

"And Marcia, she just gets upset over anything," she said. "She said she doesn't want you to dance with us anymore. But I'm sure she doesn't really mean that. There's no way she can't let you dance. It's not fair."

Heather looked up at me as she said that. I couldn't believe she would be talking to my enemies behind my back. I hadn't even left town yet.

"Staying with Tilly isn't about dance," I lied. "I need to see something new, the world outside of this town."

"What for?" she asked. "This town *is* our world. What could you possibly learn in the city that you can't learn here with me? Dance is something new. We could keep practicing and you'll get much better, you'll see."

I thought about how to tell Heather I wasn't interested in getting better at ballet.

"I won't get better," I said.

"Tash, why can't you catch a show this weekend with Tilly and then come back home like before?" Heather asked.

"Because, I just can't," I said, even though I probably could if I had wanted to. I zipped my suitcase closed, frustrated that Heather wasn't willing to think of anyone other than herself.

When Heather and I finally said good-bye, she was in tears. I waved slightly as she walked away from the house, ready to be left alone.

I stood in front of my vanity and brushed my hair out. I plugged in the curling iron. I needed to learn to do my hair on my own, especially if Tilly wouldn't do it for me while I was away. I'd never so much as seen a curling iron at her place. Her short hair had been styled in twists for years.

I pulled the first section of hair apart with my fingers and dragged the iron on top just like my mom had done so many times for me. It fell just right and so did the next two sections.

I held my left ear in with one hand and the iron in the other. I grabbed the hair and held the iron as tight as possible. I was sure to move the cord out of the sink bowl so I wouldn't electrocute myself. After awhile, I felt the heaviness of the iron weighing down my right arm and I did my best to hold it steady.

When I let go, the iron dropped right onto my ear. Immediately I felt the pain of burning flesh. I dropped the iron into the sink and pinched the ear, causing me even more pain. The tears fell freely.

I heard footsteps and knew my mom had heard the noise.

"God, Tash, what just happened?" she asked.

She looked from the iron in the sink to my ear. She pulled the cocoa butter from the cabinet under the sink and began to rub my ear. It didn't make it feel better, but I let her rub anyway.

"I was trying to do it myself since I'll be at Tilly's for so long," I told her. I took the iron carefully out of the sink and held it out for her. "Will you help me finish? I can't do it as well as you."

"Sure, let's get you fixed up," she said. She took the iron from me and hugged me tight. "My goodness, you're shaking like a leaf."

"I guess I'm just nervous," I said, drying my face with a washcloth. I let her work her magic. She redid most of my hair before speaking.

"What are you so nervous about?" my mom asked. "You've been going to stay with Tilly since you were a little girl."

"Yeah, but I've never been to Amber's Place with her," I said. "Tilly has told me stories about those girls. I don't know if I'm ready for all that."

"Nonsense, those girls are just like you," my mom said. "They have just had different life experiences."

Those girls were not like me, according to what Tilly had told me. My heart started to race just thinking about the tales of surviving on the streets.

"Don't worry, Tash," she said, "I'm actually really glad you're going to spend some time with Tilly. Maybe it is better for you to leave here for a while. We did our best to protect you from the world, but now I don't know if that was the right thing to have done for you."

"Yeah, I don't know, either," I said. She looked at me in the mirror. "I just wish Tilly wasn't so disappointed in me."

"Tilly isn't disappointed, Tash," she said. "You're growing into a young woman now. She just wants you to learn more about who you are."

I thought I knew who I was. Now I felt like I didn't know anything.

"I thought I knew that," I said.

"I know," my mom answered. "But it will be a good change for you. And having the extra time to spend in a different environment will be nice, too."

"I hope so," I said.

All of a sudden, it felt like the life I'd always known was falling apart before my very eyes and I didn't know how to stop it. My mom finished my hair and unplugged the iron. We both stared into the mirror for a while, both knowing we wouldn't see this same girl for a long, long time.

CHAPTER FOUR

SAYING GOOD-BYE WAS more difficult than I imagined.

A stranger would have thought I was moving across the country. Dad could barely get out of the car at the bus station. He handed me money and held me for a long time. My mom pulled a tissue from her purse, dabbed her eyes, and hugged me so tight I almost cried. Tilly rolled her eyes, hugged them both quickly, and boarded the bus.

"I'll miss you, Tash," Mom said. "You're going to have a great time, you'll see. And you know we'll come up to visit when we can."

I looked at her with one raised eyebrow.

"Not to shop, to see if you're okay," she said, laughing. I laughed, too. She wasn't fooling anyone. My mom wasn't going to miss any opportunity to catch some sales. "By the end of your visit, we'll be fighting to get you to come back home."

My stomach started a flip-flop exercise I was all too familiar with. It was the same pain right before I got onstage to dance, before I gave speeches in front of my English class, and the same pain before I boarded a bus to leave my parents. I leaned from one foot to the other and took a few deep breaths.

"You nervous?" she asked, giving my hand a squeeze.

I lied, shook my head, and started to gather my bags. Tilly had already taken the larger one for the driver to put underneath the bus.

"I love you," my mom mouthed to me as I walked toward the bus.

I took one step onto the bus at a time, each one slower than the one before. I could see Mom standing outside the window where Tilly had set up shop. She raised one hand and kissed it. I kissed my own hand and placed it against the window.

Tilly handed me a peppermint.

"You should always sit close to the front," Tilly said, sucking on her own candy, ignoring us, "so when you get off for the break, the driver will remember you and not leave you at some rest stop in the middle of God knows where. I've seen it happen."

I wasn't sure when or if that bit of information would be helpful to me, but I nodded to show her I got the message anyway. Knowing Tilly, she would keep talking whether I answered her or not.

"Okay, Tash, let me show you how this works," Tilly said, pulling out the bus map. I leaned on her shoulder while she excitedly pointed to each line.

"You okay over there?" she asked after she was through.

"Yeah, I'm alright," I told her, "just a little tired."

"Looks more like nerves to me," she said. "I know you're scared, but it'll work out, you'll see. This is going to be good for you."

"You really think so?" I asked. I was hoping that hearing it one more time would convince me it would be so.

"Yeah, it will, baby. You'll see," she said. She passed the map over to me and pulled out her knitting needles and yarn.

"Tilly?" I asked. "I heard what you told Mom and Dad last night. What am I supposed to learn with you?"

She put the yarn down and looked at me.

"NaTasha, I've never lied to you and I'm not about to start now," she said. "Harlem ain't nothing like what you know here. And Amber's Place is going to be quite an adjustment for you, too. Those girls have been through rough times in their short lives, things you'll never know about, thank the good Lord. Two different worlds if there ever were any. This is going to be tough, but I believe you can make it. You hear me?"

"Yes, ma'am," I said. Tilly was planning to let me tag along for a few hours each day and spend some time with the girls, helping out where I was needed.

"Girl, if you can make it through this, you'll walk out a stronger person," she said. "You trust me?"

"Yeah, Tilly, I trust you."

"Good, now help me make a grocery list. We've got a celebration to cook up tonight," she said.

Tilly celebrated everything with food. When she moved into her new apartment, instead of a housewarming, she cooked a bunch of food and invited the neighborhood.

Our list was nearly a full page long by the time the driver interrupted us. He announced we were close to a rest stop.

"Okay, folks, we are forty minutes outside of New York City and we'll be stopping soon for a break," he said over the speaker. "You will have ten minutes and ten minutes only. Please believe me when I say I will not wait for you slowpokes. If you get left out at the stop, good luck."

He laughed and set his mic down.

Tilly leaned over and said, "See, I told you." She ran through our plan of action for maximizing our rest stop time. One minute to get to the restroom and three more to use it, wash, and exit. Four minutes to stand in line and order a snack. Two to run back to the bus. She was a pro, and as soon as the bus doors opened, she was off. Her legs moved like a windup doll.

"Tilly, wait up," I called, rushing to keep up with her.

"You better catch up, girl," she said. "I'm too old to hold it for very long. Step lively."

And I stepped.

Tilly and I both deserved trophies for our record performance at the rest stop. We were back with three minutes to spare. I opened my Chocolate Delights and laughed at the other passengers running to make it back to the bus. You would have thought our driver was the ice cream man on a hot summer day. Tilly sipped her cranberry juice and shook her head, like she knew someone was about to get left behind.

The driver must have scared everyone, though, because we arrived in the city with everyone aboard. He congratulated us like we had run a marathon with everyone crossing the finish line.

"Good job, folks, it's always a pleasure when I can make a trip without losing anyone," the driver said, laughing.

He opened the undercarriage of the bus and helped us unload our bags. Times Square was just as busy as I remembered— the same amount of people, the same lights blazing, and the same sense of urgency.

"It never sleeps, huh?" I asked, to no one in particular.

"Never," the driver heard me and answered. "There's too much money to be made to sleep. Have a good time while you're here."

"Thanks," I said. "I'll try."

Tilly and I took the C train to 116th Street and Frederick Douglass Boulevard in Harlem. We stepped out onto a bustling street, near a bus depot, a small bodega, and a tire store. Darlene's Beauty Supply Shop had lines of women waiting for their turn to get their hair braided or pressed. Tilly had an extra spring in her step.

"Girl, it's good to be home," Tilly said. We walked past Darlene's and around the block to Tilly's apartment. On our way, I bought a new cell phone case and a pair of house slippers from a street vendor, because I had forgotten to pack my own. Once we unloaded our bags in her apartment, we headed to the bodega on the corner to stock Tilly's near-empty refrigerator. The store was right next to an adult video store and a small KFC.

"Did you remember my list, Tash?" Tilly asked, pulling a

mini-sized shopping cart away from the others. "We don't want to go at this all willy-nilly. We need a plan."

The store was four aisles wide. I was sure we could manage without it, but that was an unnecessary argument.

"I've got the list," I said, following behind her. Tilly is the kind of grandmother you prayed would not embarrass you in public. I had to watch her like she was the child. She was liable to say *anything* to anyone.

Our cart was half full and the list almost complete when Tilly's favorite song came on. Anthony Hamilton blared through the speakers and Tilly started having flashbacks of her nightclub days. She shook her oversized behind to the beat. I covered my laugh with my hand and looked around to make sure she wasn't scaring away any of the customers. When she finally stopped dancing, she grabbed my arm and pulled me toward the back of the bodega.

"Come on, Tash, I want you to meet my favorite meat guy," Tilly said, loudly enough for the boy around my age behind the counter to hear. He winked in our direction when he saw her coming. All of a sudden, after seeing how cute he was, I couldn't think straight. All noise around us faded— no more Anthony Hamilton, no more squeaky carts, and no more Tilly. I tucked my hair behind my ears and straightened my clothes.

"Looking good, Ms. Tilly, what can I get for you today?"

Tilly's meat guy wore his black hair cropped closely to his head. He had beautiful large brown eyes and smooth skin. I thanked God for making such a gorgeous boy. The name tag on his apron said AMIR. He smiled widely at Tilly, like she was his best customer. I wanted to be his best customer and I didn't even know him.

"Same as always, baby," Tilly told him, "but add a couple more pieces of chicken breast for me. We're celebrating tonight."

Amir went to work wrapping pieces of meat in white paper and placing the packages on his weighing scale. His muscles bulged under his white polo shirt.

"What's the celebration?" Amir asked me.

I saw his mouth and watched his eyes. In fact, I'd caught his every move since we'd walked up to the counter. So I knew he wanted me to respond, but my mouth wouldn't budge. Somehow, I'd lost my voice. My lips opened, but no sound came.

"Tash, baby?" Tilly was trying to help me out, but I still couldn't move. He was gorgeous.

I backed up when Tilly nudged me, right into a display of canned beans. The whole display toppled like bowling pins. This might have been worse than causing a collision onstage at the dance center.

"Girl, what has gotten into you?" Tilly asked, stooping to clean up my mess.

"Uh . . . I'm . . . so . . . sorry," I said, finally finding my voice.

I looked back across the counter but Amir was gone. The meat lay neatly wrapped on the scale, but I definitely scared him off. He was probably ducking behind his counter laughing hysterically or gone to grab his camera phone to snap the new girl who spilled the beans.

"Are you okay?" a deep voice asked. I felt strong arms move me out of the way of the teetering display. He wasn't behind the counter laughing at all.

"Um, yeah, I'm okay," I said, wishing I could crawl inside one of the spilled cans.

"Amir, this is my NaTasha," Tilly said proudly, despite the mess I had just made in front of her friend. She winked at him. "She's staying with me for a couple of weeks."

"Nice to meet you, NaTasha," Amir said.

"Thanks. I mean, you, too."

"Maybe I'll see you around sometime?" he asked.

Was he asking me out? I'd never even had a boy look in my direction in Adams Park. I come to visit Tilly and within hours I had the full attention of a handsome, very handsome, boy. Harlem was looking better and better by the minute.

"Yeah, maybe," I told him. Of course he'd see me around. I was already planning Tilly's next grocery list in my head and we hadn't even paid for this cartful.

Tilly giggled like this was all a part of her plan for me this summer and pushed the cart off toward the checkout counter. I followed her back to her apartment like a stray cat. She couldn't stop giggling at me. Not only was Amir probably thinking what a klutz I was, but my own grandmother was making fun of me. Tilly smiled at me and pulled on her "Grandmothers know everything" apron as soon as we walked into her kitchen. I put the groceries away while she preheated the oven.

"It isn't funny," I told her.

"Oh, yes it is and you know it, girl," she said, "but don't worry, Amir is as nice as they come. He won't hold it against you."

Yeah, right. I rolled my eyes.

Tilly's apartment looked exactly as it always did, just one step away from needing serious help from an interior decorator. Tilly had definitely gone crazy with the apple decor she loved so much. There were green and red apples painted on a border around her windowsill to match the bowl of fake apples sitting on her table, which complemented the apple place mats and teacups in her cabinets. I was always sick of apples by the time I left Tilly's place.

"The place looks good, Tilly," I told her, looking around.

It was pretty small for a one bedroom. She had a tiny kitchen with just enough space for a bar table with two stools, a living room with a nice view of the alley in between buildings, and one bathroom. I walked around, taking it all in, until I was back in the kitchen on one of Tilly's stools.

"Thank you, baby," Tilly answered. "As you can see I've been redecorating."

Before long, Tilly had macaroni and cheese baking in the oven—the real recipe with milk, eggs, and sour cream, not the Kraft noodles I usually microwaved from the box. Her collard greens were boiling on the stove. And the room smelled sweet from the apple pie sitting on the counter.

"So, Tash, this is going to be a great couple of weeks for you," Tilly said. "And I hope you'll decide to stay even longer.

It will be good to have you with me and helping out at Amber's Place."

"Okay, that's nice," I said, half listening to her, but moving toward the stove. I hovered over the greens like a watchdog, ready to pounce as soon as they were ready.

"Girl, back away from that stove before you get burned," Tilly said, pushing me away. "Why don't you set that table already? And you know to use my good china."

"Okay, Tilly," I said.

I pulled down one of her good sets, the white glass plates with a pink rose pattern around the rim, the only thing in the kitchen without apples. Tilly reached for a cup of already-used grease.

Tilly had a tendency to go overboard with a cup of grease and a frying pan. Chicken was her specialty, but she'd go as far as a fried pickle sandwich if no one stopped her. She leaned against the sink with her cup-o-nasty in one hand and a bag of flour in the other. I watched her pound the meat onto a paper towel full of flour.

She coated a wing piece and flung a dusting of flour at me. I laughed and tried to duck out of the way.

"What are you thinking about over there?" Tilly asked. "Why are you so quiet?"

"Nothing, Grandma, I'm okay," I said, hearing my mistake before I could correct it. I waited for her to explode.

Tilly turned sideways and picked up a Cutco frying pan.

"First of all, if you call me 'grandma' one more time, I'm gonna have to knock you out. Do these hips look like they belong to someone's grandmother? And secondly, I know when something is wrong with my favorite granddaughter or my name isn't Tillithia Mae Evans."

She cocked one of her heavy legs in front of the other and waved in her best Miss Black America way, the frying pan dangling in the other hand. I didn't even try to hide my laugh. She was crazy. I was her only grandchild and I'd been calling her Tilly since birth. Every time I messed up and aged her, she called me on it. Tilly wanted to be young forever.

"Nothing's wrong, Tilly," I told her. "My first impression wasn't so good today. I made such a fool of myself in front of Amir."

"Oh? You still thinking about him?" she asked, smirking.

She had to know that knocking over a canned beans display at the grocery wasn't one of my finer moments. I certainly wouldn't be able to forget about it anytime soon.

Tilly went back to the chicken and hummed "Open My Eyes, Lord" as she worked. She always hummed church songs while she cooked. Tilly once told me the Lord's angels had a direct hand in her food creations, and sometimes the angels actually seasoned her food. I listened to her hum as I set the table.

When we sat down to eat, Tilly said a quick prayer and then I scooped some greens she had boiled onto each of our plates. Tilly sat quietly and watched me.

"It wasn't so bad, Tash," Tilly said. "People knock things over at the grocery all the time."

"But I nearly took down the entire display in front of him," I said, wincing slightly at the sound of my own whining.

"Girl, please," she laughed. "You're being silly. I'm sure Amir had a good laugh and then forgot all about you."

Great, I didn't want him to forget *me*; just that I was a huge klutz.

I finished my greens and the rest of my thigh piece.

"You know you have to be ready for whatever's in store for you here?" she asked quietly. Tilly could say so much without saying much at all. I loved that about her. Working at Amber's Place wasn't going to be easy for me and we both knew it. Making a mess in front of Amir should have been the least of my worries. Walking into a teen crisis center was going to require a different type of first impression than I'd ever prepared for.

"Yeah, I know, Tilly."

Tilly handed me a wineglass and filled it with iced tea.

"Let's make a toast," she said, raising her own glass against mine, "to new beginnings and a summer full of learning and love."

After we finished eating, I cleared the dishes from the table, while Tilly started to wash. She handed me a bowl to dry.

"You have your first impression picked out for tomorrow?" she asked when we were all done. Tilly volunteered at Amber's Place four days a week. I was going to help her starting first thing in the morning.

"Yeah, I have it," I said.

"Well, go ahead and put it on," she said.

Tilly had pink curtains on her bedroom window that matched her bedspread. She was the matching queen. Her bedroom was almost as bad as her kitchen. She even had pink lining on some of the hangers in her closet. I shook my head and put on the white tank top and red skirt. I twirled around in front of the vanity mirror and waited for the tips of the skirt to catch up to me. Tilly clapped from the doorway.

"You look great, Tash," she said, "but there's something missing. I just can't put my finger on it."

She looked me over from head to toe and I did, too. Everything was in place as far as I could tell. When I turned back to look at Tilly, she held out a blue jewelry box to me.

"Tilly, you didn't have to get me anything," I told her, opening the box.

"I know it, and that's why you'll be giving these bad boys back," she said, laughing. "My mother gave these to me, I gave them to your mother, and she is passing them on to you. Hopefully, they'll bring you some luck tomorrow."

Tilly closed the clasp around my wrist of the most beautiful freshwater pearl bracelet I'd ever seen.

"Tilly," I asked, touching the pearls, "you really think I can be of help to the girls at Amber's Place?"

"I do," she said simply.

Tilly helped me get set up on the sofa in her living room. After I spoke to my parents, I pulled a knitted blanket around me and settled in for the Lifetime movie we were about to watch. Tilly hung up the phone and cuddled up next to me.

"Tash, you're gonna love it here, you'll see," she said.

I wanted so badly to believe her and to not be missing home already.

TILLY WAS UP frying eggs before the sun. I, on the other hand, wanted to stay buried under my covers for as long as I could. I wasn't ready for new faces. I didn't want to make new friends. What if I couldn't make friends? Maybe the girls would like me right away. But maybe they wouldn't.

I spent an abnormal amount of time in the shower, until Tilly knocked on the door to get me out. I really felt like hiding in the bathroom all day. Getting dressed was a chore. My deodorant did me no good. Sweat beads formed around my arms and my hairline. Every time I managed to calm down, it would start all over again.

I finished putting on my first impression outfit and looked at myself in the mirror. I tried my deep breathing routine, just like the one I used before going onstage to dance. Only it wasn't working properly. My body knew I wasn't going onstage today, at least not to dance.

Tilly called me to eat breakfast. I fixed a plate of cheese eggs, two pieces of bacon, and wheat toast with strawberry jelly, and sat across from her. She sipped her Earl Grey tea with milk and sugar and glanced every now and then at her Timex.

"We've got to hurry, baby, if we're going to catch space on the train," she said. I folded the eggs and bacon inside the bread like a sandwich. I took four big bites. I chewed my food fast like laundry in a spin cycle.

"I'm ready when you are, Tilly," I said, brushing a few crumbs off of my chin.

We cleaned the dishes together and turned all the lights off. I followed her out. On the way out of the building I almost tripped over an old man lying across the stairs. He rolled out of his sleeping spot and stretched an arm toward me after I bumped him. I grabbed Tilly's arm, pushed her back inside the building, and slammed the front door closed.

"Call the police, Tilly," I said frantically. She squeezed past me and looked through the peephole to see outside. She rolled her eyes and pinched my cheek.

"Tilly, this is not funny, he could hurt us," I said.

"Girl, that's Rex, he lives on this block," Tilly said, wiping her tears from laughing so hard.

"Exactly where on the block?" I asked. "Did he forget his keys or something?"

Tilly ignored me and pushed the door open. She kicked Rex playfully in the back. He moved out of the way and looked around to see who had hit him for the second time.

"Hey, there, Ms. Tilly," he said, coughing into his arm. "How you doing this beautiful morning?"

"We're fine, Rex," Tilly said, walking down the steps past

him. "I done told you about sleeping on my stoop. You're gone make me fall one of these days."

"Alright, Ms. Tilly," Rex said. "I'm up."

Rex rolled the rest of the way down the stairs and popped up at the bottom with a smile on his face. He leaned on a shopping cart, which looked like an apartment on wheels, then began to search through a bag. He had a mountain of blankets, plastic bags, newspapers, and shoes all inside the one cart. He caught me staring and stuck out his hand.

"I'm Rex," he said, "and who might you be?"

His hands looked ashy, rough, and cracked, like he was employed at a construction site, except not the employed part. There was dirt under every fingernail and he smelled. I didn't want to shake hands. I grabbed a finger of his in my own and smiled.

"I'm NaTasha, Tilly's granddaughter," I told him. Tilly motioned for me to keep walking, so I waved to Rex and we kept going.

Rex was still yelling after Tilly all the way down the block, something about bringing him a newspaper. Although, to me, it looked like he had plenty stacked in the basket underneath his cart. Every few steps I looked back to see if Rex was still behind us.

"He's harmless, Tash, no need to worry," Tilly said. "Rex is a war veteran and a good man. Now, he's just down on his luck is all."

The sun was out and so was everyone in the neighborhood. Women pushed baby strollers. Men in suits dodged one another on the sidewalk. People poured in and out of the sub-way station. Tilly kept the pace of a track star all the way to the nearest train station. I struggled to keep up.

We swiped our subway cards and waited on the platform. A few times Tilly eyed her watch and leaned across the yellow caution line, looking for the train.

"Tilly, be careful," I said. "Please don't fall down there. I don't know how I would get you back up again."

"Oh, you wouldn't be able to get me up, but I won't fall," she said. "Stay back, though. We know how graceful you can be when you get nervous."

"Real funny, Tilly," I said, smiling.

I was surprised how many people were waiting for the same train. The lines on the platform got longer each minute, and I was sure not everyone would fit on. A man pushed past me and almost knocked me close to the yellow line. I grabbed Tilly and took a deep breath. I wondered if anyone had ever fallen on the tracks before.

"Train will be here any minute," Tilly said. She held on to me with one hand and stepped forward to look for the train again.

I stood clear of the edge until our uptown train rattled to a stop. We shuffled onto the train and stood near the center of the crowded car. An older black woman pushing a stroller sat down in front of me and pulled out a newspaper. The little blond girl in the stroller finished off a bag of Doritos and poured the crumbs into her mouth and all over her lap. The older woman didn't notice or pretended not to. On the other side of Tilly, a young couple hugged each other tightly, closed their eyes, and leaned against each other.

"Tilly, how many stops are we going?" I asked after we'd been riding for what felt like fifteen minutes.

"The Bronx is a few more stops, baby," she said.

"Amber's Place is in the Bronx? But I thought you always said the Bronx is too dangerous," I said. Tilly smiled and patted the back of my hand.

"It's not that dangerous if you know where you're going," she said, "and you'll be fine with me, don't worry."

I was worried. Suddenly, the train went above ground. Light poured into the subway car. A little boy a few seats from me swung a Spider-Man doll up in the air. I listened to a baby crying, a woman coughing, and a couple laughing. A few riders walked through to other cars while the train was still in motion.

"Tilly, has anyone gotten stuck in the doors before?"

"Yeah, baby, I'm sure they have," she said, "but usually the doors will open right up and the operator will yell to stand clear of the door. But folks are always running late and trying to step in at the last minute. Watch and you'll see."

I did see.

A few stops later a tall lady stuck her cane in between the doors and waited for them to open before pushing herself in. A group of boys my age took their time boarding and held the doors until each one of their friends could run inside. Other riders started complaining, but the boys just laughed.

I leaned my head back against the seat when I got tired of people watching. The woman next to me turned her head toward me and sneezed right into my ear. I frowned, wiped my ear, and scooted closer to Tilly. The woman took a tissue from the stroller and wiped her mouth then offered me the same tissue. I shook my head. My stomach started to ache again, a bit from the anticipation but mostly from the new germs probably swirling around in my body.

"Are we almost there, Tilly?" I asked. "I don't think I can take much more."

"Three more stops," she said.

The doors opened at Tremont Avenue and Tilly pulled me out of the train car. I was so happy to have fresher air.

"I can't believe people ride this far every day," I told Tilly as we walked down the stairs to ground level. "Why doesn't everyone just drive?"

"Could you imagine what the streets would look like if every one of these people were behind the wheel of a car?" she said, giggling. "Child, it would be a mess."

Tilly was right. Driving would be a complete disaster. We filed down the stairs and waited in a long line to leave through revolving doors. We exited the subway station and into a whole new world.

Three men in heavy coats stood on the corner throwing dice into a pile of money. A chubby baby wearing only a diaper wobbled nearby holding on to a bottle of milk. A woman, looking like she belonged with the baby, talked loudly on a cell phone about a clothing sale down the block. An old man, wearing a brown-and-white pin-striped suit, tried to sell Tilly a griddle iron. She told him no and pulled me down the block past him.

"Don't stare, girl," she hissed. "It's rude. Just keep on walking."

I couldn't help it. There were so many people in the street. A girl around my age reached for my hand and offered to braid my hair for twenty-five dollars. A hairy kid wearing khaki pants and a baggy, sleeveless sweatshirt wanted Tilly to buy a leather briefcase, but she said no. At every corner someone offered us something: socks, toothbrushes, books for one dollar, and all kinds of toys. We did stop for grapes from a fruit stand.

"Okay, here we are," Tilly said, walking up the sidewalk to what looked like an old warehouse. My heart skipped a few beats.

"Amber's Place is in a warehouse?" I asked.

"Hush, come on, you'll see," she said.

The crisis center looked like a factory out of operation. A large billboard with torn lettering stood on the lawn by the front door warning intruders of prosecution. Three rows of bars stretched across every window and a security guard came out to pat us down before we entered. Apparently, one girl's boyfriend refused recently to comply with the "no weapons" policy. I followed Tilly through the metal detectors anyway.

Tilly placed her jacket, the bag of grapes, and her pocketbook on the table in front of the guard and passed quickly through the buzzer. I tried to follow after putting my own purse down, but the bell rang, and the guard stopped me with his big arms.

The guard searched through my makeup, a small wad of cash, and my school ID. And then he held up a small pocketknife. My hands went straight to my mouth. My mom must have slipped that in when I wasn't looking.

"What in the hell are you doing carrying a knife, girl?" Tilly hissed through the space in her top front teeth.

"I'll give you one guess," I told her.

I hoped the guard wouldn't take me away. Instead, he sent me back through the detector and frisked me, picking through each pocket and even opening the waistband of my skirt. There had to be some limit to the amount of embarrassment a girl had to take in one week. I was going into a crisis center as a volunteer, not getting on an international flight.

"That couldn't have been anybody but your momma," Tilly said, shaking her head. "I should have known."

I nodded. My mom had slipped it in my bag along with her credit card. I'm sure she was only looking out for me and didn't have any intention of bailing me out of this place.

"What kinds of girls need a security guard anyway?" I asked. "Did you bring me to some secret jail, Tilly?"

The guard kept my knife but waved me through. As soon as we were past security, Tilly looked excited again.

The inside of the building looked nothing like the outside of Amber's Place. The walls were pale blue and had a flower trim that matched the sofas lining the walls. Small circular tables were spread in the center of the large main room. Girls were everywhere. There must have been hundreds: dark skinned, light skinned, white, Hispanic, black, Indian, Asian, girls with dreadlocks, cornrows, straight hair, curly hair, short girls, tall girls. I felt like we were at some kind of women's expo or multicultural convention. I stood with my mouth wide open, looking at each one of them.

"What does she think this is? A circus?" a small Indian girl with a bob cut asked.

No one answered her but the two girls with her laughed and stared back at me. I closed my mouth and caught up to Tilly, who had crossed the room.

The girls chatted in small groups. Some were sitting, some were lying on pillows, and in one corner of the room others stood against the walls. They all seemed to be waiting for something to happen. A large TV played an episode of *Jerry Springer* and three girls yelled at the TV as if they were a part of the show.

"Get her, girl," one of the girls shouted, as one TV guest punched the other in the face. "That's what she gets for messing with your man."

I pulled Tilly to the side.

"Do you know all these girls?" I whispered.

Only a few of the girls looked like my friends from home. One girl even resembled Heather, which made me sad, and reminded me of my promise to call her as often as I could.

"Come on, I want you to meet someone," Tilly said.

We walked through the sea of girls, who parted only a little as we came through. I could feel their eyes on me like little lasers. Most of the conversations quieted and even stopped as we passed by.

"Hey, Tilly," one of the girls called out.

"Hey, Martine," Tilly replied to a beautiful Hispanic girl

with long black hair. The girl approached, inspecting me up and down like the security guard. She smacked her gum and hugged Tilly, keeping her eyes on me.

"How you been doing, girl?" Tilly asked her.

"Same old shit and you know I'm trying to be anywhere but here," Martine said. A few of the girls around Martine laughed and so did Tilly. She actually cursed and my grandmother didn't swing at her. I was amazed. I had no idea how Tilly was so familiar with these girls, but one of them just got away with murder.

We kept walking until we reached a long gray hallway lined with doors. On each door was an inspirational poster, like "Life has a way of knocking at your door; be sure you're ready to open it." Tilly knocked on the second door on the right and turned the knob.

"Inez, you in there?" Tilly called.

"Tilly, is that you?" a woman answered.

"You know it's me, Red," Tilly said. "I have someone I want you to meet."

"She's a character, you'll love her," Tilly whispered to me. "Her name is Inez, but we all call her Red."

A woman Tilly's age opened the door and pulled us inside with both hands. She reminded me of a cartoon character, the fire engine red hair with one blond strip was killing me. She wore a warm smile and had chubby cheeks.

"*Dios mío*, if this isn't Miriam's daughter, I don't know who is," the woman said. She was a pretty woman. She wore a black suit that matched her glasses and black heels. Even with the heels she only came right below my shoulders.

Tilly and the woman hugged. Then the woman hugged me tightly. For a small person, she was pretty strong. I looked at Tilly and waited for the air to start flowing back into my lungs.

"Tash, Red knows your mother from when she was a little girl," Tilly said. "We all used to come by to help at Amber's Place. It's like a second home to our family."

The idea of my mom growing up in Harlem was hard enough to picture. The idea of her volunteering in a place like this was unimaginable.

"Red, this is NaTasha, she's staying with me for a few weeks," Tilly said. "She's going to help us out here. If you need her, just holler. NaTasha, this is Red, she's saved a lot of lives here over the years."

"Together, we've saved lives," Red interjected quickly, turning to me. "Don't let your grandmother fool you. I don't do it alone. Tilly has been volunteering here for more years than I have been around."

"Okay, it hasn't been that long, since I'm only twenty-seven," Tilly said with her insulted face. We all laughed at that. She could probably pass for forty-seven, though.

"We're about to get started. Are you both going to stay around for a while today?" Red asked, grabbing a notebook from her desk. We nodded and followed her back out into the circus.

CHAPTER SIX

RED STOOD ON a stool, raised her notebook high in the air, and waved it like a magic wand. What looked like fairy dust came floating down, but Red actually hit a dusty ceiling fan while waving the book above her head. The girls laughed as she dodged the dirt falling on her.

"Girls, I need you in your groups now, please," Red announced. The girls dispersed to several round tables in the room and filled the seats.

"What's going on?" I whispered to Tilly. She mouthed "group time" and motioned for me to stick close to Red. I don't know what I expected, but I knew she couldn't hold my hand all day.

Tilly winked at me and then joined a group across the room, leaving me alone in the center like a ringmaster. The girls watched and waited to see what tricks, if any, I had up my sleeve.

"Girls, I want to introduce you to Tilly's granddaughter, NaTasha," Red said, coming to my rescue.

I heard the giggles. I wanted to hide or disappear or die or something just so I wasn't on display. I felt the girls watching me. No one said hello or moved to introduce themselves. I just stood there and tried not to make eye contact too much. My skin felt all tingly, like a mosquito kept landing on me and wouldn't quit. Red pulled me toward a group of girls near the front of the room and sat me down in the circle of chairs.

"Where she think she was going dressed like that?" a darkskinned girl asked the group as soon as I was seated. She had the darkest skin I had ever seen. She pushed her millions of tiny braids behind her back and propped both hands on her hips like she was posing for a picture. I was the idiot who wore a nice new skirt to a miniprison. Baggy jeans and a white T-shirt was the outfit of choice for most of them. I hadn't even gotten close. Why didn't Tilly tell me? I wanted to melt right into the floor.

"She thought we was ballroom dancing today, huh, Quiana?" said a Hispanic girl with thick, curly hair pulled up in a ponytail on the top of her head. She stood up and started to salsa right there in front of me. The whole circle started laughing.

"Yeah, except we don't ballroom," Quiana answered her. She bent over and shook her backside into the girl with the ponytail. Red and I were the only ones who didn't find their joke funny. Tilly was too far away to defend me.

Red held up her notebook and I hoped she would throw it at them or ship them off to another group. No luck. They sat back down in the two chairs directly across from me and smiled slyly.

"Hey," the girl on my left whispered. She was looking behind her chair like she dropped something. I turned to help her search for whatever it was.

"Hey, yourself," I whispered back.

"Shh . . . don't let Red hear you," she said and rolled her large blue eyes around and around like pool balls rolling on a table. "She hates when we talk out of turn during group time."

"Oh, okay," I said quietly, glancing at Red but leaning closer to the girl with the eyes.

"I just wanted to say hi, that's all," she said. She shifted her eyes toward the floor and smiled sweetly. She was a plump girl with pale skin and thin black hair to her shoulders. I relaxed a little and smiled at her. She closed her eyes and wrapped her arms around her stomach like her breakfast would come back up at any moment. I scooted back toward Red.

"Okay, ladies, today we're talking about regret and rebuilding," she said loudly for all the groups to hear. "Share with your group one regret and one way you plan to rebuild from this regret. Let's state our rules of discussion out loud please."

"Share, respect, and take turns," the girls yelled together. The room erupted as the girls chanted. Their voices sounded like a hundred balloons popping one after the other.

As soon as the assignment was given and the chant was over, the girls started to chatter. I was happy to have the attention off of me for a while. I looked around for Tilly. She was seated in a circle across the room, three groups away from my own.

Tilly caught my eye and waved. I waved and turned back to my group. Quiana and her dancing friend waved mockingly at me, too. I smiled weakly and lifted a shaking hand. They shoved each other and started laughing again.

"Who would like to start us off, ladies?" Red asked.

"Well, I regret getting knocked up," a girl on my right blurted out. So much for not talking out of turn. "No one told me it would feel like this."

Her stomach nearly reached her knees like the baby could come at any moment.

"Okay, Maria, tell us more about your regret," said Red, writing something on her pad. When she wasn't writing, Red rubbed her hands together or pushed her hair behind her ears or rocked her body like she was in a recliner.

"I mean, I'm going to love her and everything, but I can't go with my friends no more and I can't hang out with my baby's daddy like I used to," she said. "If I would have waited, maybe things would be different, you know? I wouldn't have to go to the doctor every day and I could just kick it again."

"You was having too much fun under them sheets," Quiana said and slapped hands with the Hispanic girl next to her. They both laughed. "Should have thought about that earlier, *mami*."

"Shut up, Quiana," Maria told her. "I know that already. That's why I'm talking about it, stupid."

"Ladies, please remember to respect one another and wait for your turn," Red said. "We don't want to make anyone feel uncomfortable here."

Too late. I shouldn't be hearing these kinds of things from people I didn't even know. I was here to help, so I sure hoped Red didn't expect me to share. I looked back at Tilly, but she was in full conversation, not looking at me.

"Okay, so, Maria, what have you learned from that regret?" Red asked. "What do you plan on doing to not make that same regret again?"

"I learned to keep my legs closed," Maria answered, encouraging the other girls to laugh with her while she held her stomach tightly. "And Carlos will just have to wait."

The other girls laughed and reached to feel Maria's belly. Quiana glared at me the whole time. I smiled along with the other girls. At least the lesson was learned. I imagined life with a baby in my arms. I couldn't even survive a day by myself without help, let alone taking care of another human being.

"Who would like to go next?" Red asked, flipping to the next page on her pad. She elbowed a tall Hispanic girl with dirty-blond hair. "Monique? How about you? You usually have a lot to share with us."

Monique adjusted her halter top so we could no longer see her purple lace bra, and started talking about stealing money from her mother's purse.

"I only took it so I could party with my girls," she said, smirking. "She wouldn't have known if I didn't trip over her on my way out the door."

Monique looked upset for a moment, but then started laughing. Her laugh was muffled, though, like someone was holding a hand over her mouth. A couple of the girls joined in but a few looked around at one another, confused. Red, too.

"Um . . . Monique, do you mean tripped over something near your mother?" Red asked.

"Nah, Monique's momma drinks as much as my parents do," a dark-skinned girl with shoulder-length hair added, pushing Monique on the shoulder. "Where you think *she* learned to drink like that from?"

Red shifted back and forth in her chair.

"So, Monique, what did you learn from this?" she asked.

"Next time, I'm gonna wait until I know she's passed out good," Monique said, amusing her friends. She caught Red writing something down on her paper and held her hand against her heart and bowed her head. "I mean, I'm not gonna steal and I'm gonna try to quit drinking."

I didn't belong here, among these girls. How was I supposed to help with any of this? These stories were straight from the talk shows, stories that weren't even real. Red caught my eye and my heart started beating fast. I really hoped she wasn't going to ask me to say anything.

"You have to mean the words, not just say them, for them to matter," Red told the group. "Otherwise, we're wasting our time here. You all know the mistakes I made at your age—sex, drugs, stealing, detention centers, and even assault. It wasn't pretty, but I've turned myself around and we're here so that you will recognize you can do the same."

The girls were finally quiet.

"NaTasha, we know you're visiting, but I'd like to give you the opportunity to share if you'd like," Red said after awhile. "We all have issues and sometimes it's easier to talk about them and get them off your chest. Everything said in this circle stays in this circle, just to let you know."

The girls waited and glared.

I was perfectly okay with all of the issues on my chest. I didn't need to share, want to share, nor was I going to share. I wasn't one of these girls. I didn't have problems like they said they had. They would roll on the floor laughing at my problems. Well, they could wait all night if they wanted. I crossed my arms and waited patiently for Red to move on.

The girls exploded.

"Hey, I thought we had to share, Red," the girl with big, blue eyes shouted out.

"Yeah, so what's your story, huh?" Maria said, looking at me. "You don't get to sit here and listen to my shit and then act like you're all holier-than-thou. I don't think so."

"You think you're better than us, *pretty* girl?" Quiana asked. Quiana sat with her elbows on her knees, challenging me to stay quiet. I still didn't open my mouth. I had forgotten anything that I might have shared anyway. No one had ever called me pretty before, sarcastically or not. "She does think she's better than us, girls. She isn't from here and she isn't like us and she doesn't *care* nothing about us."

"Ladies, that's enough," Red finally interrupted, waving the notebook in front of Quiana like a white flag. "It's her first day with us. Maybe she'll want to share tomorrow."

Fat chance.

I didn't speak the entire train ride home. I closed my eyes and pretended to sleep and Tilly let me. I didn't want to have to tell her I wasn't going back to Amber's Place. I didn't want to disappoint her already.

When we got back to Tilly's neighborhood, I convinced her to let me walk around alone for a while. I wanted to think about the day and all the things I'd heard. At first, Tilly insisted on going with me, but I told her I really needed to be alone. She looked hurt, but gave in after a few minutes, and made sure I kept her house key and a couple of dollars on me.

"You be careful, you hear me?" Tilly asked. "This is not the countryside and nobody around here cares that you are from there, either. So put that sweet and innocent face in your pocketbook for a while."

I passed by Hope Baptist, Tilly's home church, which seemed like everyone's home church in this neighborhood. I knew I would be seeing the inside of that building many times before I went home. Fine by me, since it looked like I would need God's help to get me through the next few weeks.

It was a perfect afternoon to be walking, a slight breeze, warm, and no humidity. Not too many people were out for a leisurely stroll, though. One lady shoved me out of her way as she sped by. A boy about my age yelled for me to move as he rolled by on his skateboard. I inhaled car fumes, dog urine, and leftover food spilled on the street. I was happy to be out, though, out of Tilly's reach, out of a ballet dancer's nightmare, out of a circle of troubled teen girls, out of the line of fire.

I walked past a skinny Asian woman who held a sign about her losing a job and needing money to feed her two kids. I dropped one of my dollars into her cardboard box, even though Tilly had said not to. She said some people choose to live on the street and have more money stored than she'll have in her whole lifetime. Not sure I believed that. The woman thanked me and I kept walking.

I rounded another corner and stopped to watch a basketball game in progress. The boys on the court were serious, like a cash prize was on the line. Some had their shirts pulled over their heads, some only wore basketball shorts, and one boy had on a sweat suit. Curse words poured from the boys as they ran back and forth across their concrete court.

After the third basket slammed into the wire-rimmed hoop, I turned around to continue walking and smacked right into someone. The boy's soda flew out of his hand and hit the sidewalk, spilling out all over. I covered my mouth with my hand and looked up to see who I had assaulted.

"Yo, watch where you're going," the boy said angrily. Some of the drink had sprayed his dreadlocks. He wiped his hair with the sleeve of his shirt. "I don't even have any more change."

"I'm really sorry, I didn't see you standing there," I told him.

He stared at me for a moment like he was thinking of mean things to say. Then his frown loosened a bit and his hazel eyes shone brightly.

"Hey, you better slow your roll around here, girl," he warned me. "The next guy you run into may not know who you are and bump you right back."

"Well, I said I was sorry," I snapped back, "and *you* don't know me."

"Yeah, well, just remember what I said," he told me.

"It won't happen again," I said. I put up my hands in surrender and he smiled. I moved away from him and started walking back toward Tilly's apartment building.

"Hey, you! Wait up!" he yelled.

I thought, *Oh, great, now I have a stalker.* Tilly would be pissed. I was not supposed to talk to anyone or attract any unwanted attention. So much for that plan. I kept going, walking a little faster. Tilly's apartment was straight ahead on the next block. If I could make it to the corner, I was home free.

"Hey, NaTasha, don't you remember me?" my stalker called out.

I stopped my speed walk abruptly and turned around, completely going against Tilly's rules of survival.

"How do you know my name?" I asked him, crossing my arms.

"NaTasha, it's me, Khalik," he said, pulling all of his dreadlocks behind his back with one hand. He looked me right in the eyes and cocked his head to the side like he was posing for the cover of *GQ*. Something about him was vaguely familiar, but I couldn't place his face.

"I live in Tilly's building," he said, releasing his hair. "We used to hang when we were younger."

I remembered having friends here when I was younger, but this broad-shouldered, handsome boy couldn't have been one of them. This boy had round eyes and high cheekbones. And he smelled amazing, like a warm chocolate brownie with caramel icing and a scoop of vanilla ice cream on top. The brown-and-white Sean John T-shirt he was wearing matched the brown-and-white Adidas sneakers on his feet. He was tall enough to be out on the court with the other ball players. He pulled a brown stretchy headband from the pocket of his pants and gathered his hair back again. He must have been growing that hair for years.

"I think you have the wrong person," I told him, turning back around to head home.

"I remember a little girl who screamed anytime Tilly tried to braid her hair," he said to my back. I slowed down but kept my back to him while he continued. "This little girl would only play with me and she always had to choose the game. I always wanted to play ball, but she always wanted to play house or jump rope or something. It usually had something to do with a little white baby doll with blond hair that never left her arms."

Khalik had grown up.

I turned around to look at him again and smiled, breaking yet another one of Tilly's rules. My childhood crush I used to tell Heather about had transformed into a man, a good-looking man.

"You've changed, Khalik," I told him, sizing him up again.

"You think so?" Khalik asked, moving closer to me than I should have let him, according to the rules. He looked me up and down and moved another step closer, eyeing my skirt and lingering on a spot where my stomach was peeking out below my tank top. "You too."

"Not *that* much," I told him, taking a step backward and pulling down on my top.

"Oh . . . you mean you still carry that ratty old white doll around?" he asked, laughing and searching around me for the doll.

"No, I guess I have changed a little," I said, backing up a few more steps. "So, how's your life? What have you been up to?"

"I'm out of school for the summer and just hanging out with my boys. You know how it is," he said. I wished I knew. I wanted to be home hanging out with my own friends. "What about you? You here for a quick weekend in the city?"

"Actually, I'll be here for a few weeks this time," I told him. "You still live in the building?"

"Yeah, I'm headed there now," he said. "How's Ms. Tilly?"

"Still cooking up a storm, as usual," I told him. "I'll tell her you said hello."

We turned to walk the rest of the way together to the

building. It was just starting to get dark. Knowing Tilly, she was probably watching us from her window and had been the whole time, which would explain why she hadn't come for me yet.

Khalik opened the front door and held it for me to pass through.

"So, maybe we can catch up before you leave," he said, stepping inside behind me. The memory of us holding hands, and roller skating on the very floor we were standing on, came to me and I laughed out loud. Khalik looked hurt. "Alright, Tash, you ain't got to be rude about it, I was just asking."

"No, no, I mean, yes," I said, hiding my smile. "I was just remembering us skating on this floor. You used to fall all the time."

Khalik started laughing, too.

"Nah, the way I remember it, you were the one always bustin' your ass," he said. He caught my eye and smiled. "Hey, I'll catch you later then, Tash."

"Okay, good night," I told him, and started up the stairs.

When I got in, Tilly was on the phone. I reached for my cell phone right away to call Heather. I couldn't wait to tell her about the encounter I just had with Khalik.

"You remember that guy I used to tell you about?" I asked Heather. "You know, the one that lived in Tilly's building?"

Khalik is the only boy I ever really told her I liked, other than Matt Billings.

"Let me guess, you saw him, and you're getting married and never coming back?" she said.

"You got it, and we may elope," I told her.

"NaTasha!"

"Just kidding, but if he did ask me, I'd have to think long and hard about my decision," I told her. "How are things in Adams Park? Are you dying of boredom yet?"

I could picture Heather lying faceup on her bed, staring at her own star stickers.

"Well, actually, I have some big news for you," she said. "Matt is throwing a party in a few weeks and he asked me to invite you." When Heather got excited, all her words slurred like she'd had too much to drink. The news spilled out of her mouth like water from a fountain.

"*Who* is having a party?" I said, interrupting her.

"Tash, what other Matt do you know?" Heather squealed. "And, get this, he asked if I had ideas for a theme!"

Matt Billings called Heather to invite us to a party. That was *huge* news.

"Wait," I said. "Why didn't he call me himself if he wanted to invite me to a party?"

"Oh, you know how guys are," Heather answered. "They run into one friend and ask for all her friends. You're missing the point, Tash. We are going to Matt Billings's party!"

Matt must not have heard about the dance recital at all. He would never invite me to a party if he had heard what happened to Stephanie. Maybe I could show my face in Adams Park after all. I was hiding out in Harlem being laughed at by a bunch of delinquents while my best friend was enjoying my summer vacation at home talking on the phone and planning a party with *my* Matt Billings.

"Tash?"

"I don't know, Heather, I'll have to call you back," I said. "I may be busy getting married that weekend."

TILLY CONVINCED ME to give the girls at Amber's
Place another chance. *I told you it wasn't going to be easy,* she
reminded me.

We headed into the center, and I hoped share time wasn't
a regular thing. But when we got there the girls were already
in their groups and were beginning to share. I looked at Tilly
for a way out, but she nodded to my group and walked toward
her own.

"Hey, Tash, welcome back," Red announced as soon as she
saw me. "We're going around the circle and telling everyone
one thing we hate about ourselves. Join us."

Like I had a choice. Where else was I going to go? Tilly
had brought me about as far north as you could go on the subway and I couldn't find my way back if I wanted to.

I sat down next to the girl who had hugged her stomach
during the last session. She had her black hair pulled into a
ponytail high on her head, accentuating her big, blue eyes.
She smiled weakly at me. Her skin was sweaty and pale
like Elmer's school glue. I wondered if she had the flu or
something.

"Okay, Susan, go ahead, you can continue," Red said, pointing to the pasty-skinned girl.

Susan moved her hands from her stomach and put them on both her cheeks and stared between her feet. All the girls in the circle followed her gaze to the floor.

"I hate my feet," she said quietly. "And I hate my knees, and my fat thighs and the extra flab around my belly, the way my skin swings on my elbows when I move my arms, and my saggy boobs."

The girls around her began to giggle until they saw the tears falling from her eyes. Her sadness was like a wave of gloom that hit us all at the same time. She was serious. The only body parts she left out were from the neck up. I wondered if she was happy with anything up there. I didn't think so.

"Susan, that's quite a list," Red said, flipping pages in her notebook. She scooted to the front of her seat to touch Susan's knee. "You only had to give us one, and I hope at some point you're able to come to grips with your body. We all do at some point in our lives."

The girls were oddly quiet. None of the taunts or insults thrown at the previous session was happening. All eyes were on Red. Susan had tear after tear running down her cheeks. She didn't try to fight them back at all.

"I'm not finished," she said quietly, interrupting Red, who withdrew her hand and motioned for Susan to continue. All eyes went back to Susan again. "I also hate having a boyfriend who hates all of these things about me, too."

She wrapped her arms back around her stomach. I thought about putting my arm around Susan's shoulders. I would do that for a friend. But these girls weren't my friends. Susan would move away from me if I tried to comfort her. Touching was probably breaking some rule I didn't know about anyway.

"Girls, we're doing this exercise so that you can release any of your anxiety or negative feelings," Red said. "I'm hoping the act of saying our fears and hates aloud will free you in some way. Susan, would you like to reflect anymore?"

Susan shook her head. She probably wouldn't talk ever again for the rest of her life. In fact, her honesty had silenced everyone in the group. I glanced around our circle again. Susan wasn't the only one with tears in her eyes. I lowered my head and prayed for the uncomfortable silence to disappear. I would have even welcomed the new-girl jokes to make this tension go away.

"Rochelle, why don't you go next," Red said, shifting in her seat to face the girl on Susan's other side.

Rochelle pulled her thick, shoulder-length hair behind her ears and leaned back in her seat. She looked more ready to sleep than to share with a group about her feelings. I watched her eyeball each member of the group before starting.

"I hate my parents," she said, wiping an invisible hair from her face. "I hate that my mom was strung out and my daddy wasn't never around and jumped in and out of jail. I hate them for making me. When I was little I swore I wouldn't be nothing like them, but look at me. I'm just like them. I hate when people see me coming and they grab their stuff like I'm gonna steal something or when I'm in a store and the salespeople walk right past me like I don't need no help finding nothing. I hate a lot of things."

Red rocked slowly like this information was heavier than she expected. I wanted her to say something soothing, but she just kept rocking back and forth.

"Does anyone want to speak to Rochelle?" she asked after awhile.

No one moved. No one spoke. No one looked around. Susan was still hunched over, wiping tears from her eyes. Quiana looked like a mannequin, stiff and unaffected. The other girls just listened.

"You're here, aren't you?" I asked quietly. My mouth obviously wasn't following directions from my brain, which only happened at the most inopportune times like this one.

Rochelle looked surprised. "What?"

"Well, you said you're like your parents, but you're not in jail like them, you're here with us," I stated. "Maybe you aren't as similar to them as you think."

Red smiled and nodded her head in agreement with me. Rochelle wasn't as impressed. Her sad face quickly turned sour. She glared at me like I was the one who had just said all those bad things about her family members. I immediately regretted getting involved.

"I just got out, new girl," she said, snapping at me. "And when I go home tonight, I'm going past the drug dealers on my street and the hustlers trying to pimp me out and my parents' friends crashing at our place because they got kicked out of their own. I'm just like them."

I thought of Tilly's apartment with its matching decor and the quiet and the comfort.

"I just thought . . ." I started.

"I know what you thought, NaTasha," Rochelle stopped me, "and you don't know nothing about me or my life or any-one else's in here for that matter. No one in here comes from the cushy stuck-up suburbs and no one here lives the perfect life you do, so I don't even know why you're here."

All the girls looked at me now. Even Susan.

"Sorry," I told her.

"Yeah," Rochelle said.

Thankfully, Red didn't miss a beat. "We all have different experiences in our lives, no matter where we come from. NaTasha does come from a different place, but we all have problems," Red said. She had stopped rocking and turned to me. "Maybe, NaTasha, you'd like to share with the girls some-thing you hate."

I didn't, but I had to dig myself out of the grave I'd just dug with Rochelle. The girls wanted blood and I knew it. Every eye was on me. They wouldn't let me get away with the silent treatment today. No way.

My head started to pound. I smoothed my jeans, glancing up at all the eyes watching me. My heartbeat was in my throat. The girls were waiting.

"Sometimes, I hate the color of my skin."

As soon as the words came out of my mouth, I knew I was in trouble. It was a shock even to me. I had never said them out loud, even though I'd felt it my whole life.

Susan gasped and stared at the others to see what they'd do. Quiana grinned and folded her arms across her chest, happy to have some dirt against me. Rochelle leaned forward and popped her knuckles and challenged me to a staring contest that I didn't want to participate in. Red rocked back and forth for a while before speaking. She closed her eyes and took a deep breath.

"Thank you, NaTasha, I know how difficult that was for you," Red said. "Can anyone offer an encouraging word?"

Silence. My whole body was hot and I needed a blast of fresh air right away. When it was clear no one else was interested in holding a conversation, especially to give nice words to me, Red dismissed us for the day. I ran out of the circle toward the exit faster than I knew I could move.

If I knew anything about Quiana and Rochelle, they would have the word out at Amber's Place by the end of the day. Confidentiality my ass. My group had no loyalty to the new girl. After hearing their own stories, it was clear those girls knew nothing about following the rules.

It was only a matter of time before every girl at the center would know my greatest secret. Tilly would be heartbroken. I had to find her.

When I found Tilly I didn't know what to say. I couldn't tell her about the silence I had created at the end of our session. Or the dirty looks I'd gotten as a result of my confession.

"Hey, baby, how was group today?" Tilly asked, hugging me tight. She hadn't heard yet. "These girls go through some stuff, don't they? Many wouldn't have a chance if it wasn't for this place."

I wasn't sure what I was doing here, besides giving the girls something to take their minds off their own issues. I was the bait and they were the hungry fish at the bottom of the sea. I couldn't believe I fell into their trap.

"It was fine," I said, with my head down. "But I just want to go home."

Tilly probably thought I meant her apartment, but what I really wanted more than anything was to go *home* home. And the more I thought about Matt and Heather planning a party together without me, the more I was sure I should be volunteering my time helping Matt Billings plan his party instead of spending time with these hateful girls at Amber's Place. They didn't want me around and I didn't want to be here.

"Tash, you'll mean more to these girls than you even know, so don't give up just now," Tilly said.

I thought about how good it would feel to get my things and run out of here.

"Baby," Tilly continued, "this place helped your mother when she tried to drop out of school, it helped me when I was down and out, and I'm hoping it will help you, too."

Tilly said some girls started waiting for my mom after school. They would pull her hair and tear at her clothes like she was a rag doll. Tilly told me it got so bad, my mom wanted to drop out of school, but Tilly wouldn't hear of it. They talked it over and went searching for Amber's Place, the only safe haven at the time for girls like my mom. Tilly was forever grateful and had been volunteering there ever since.

That all sounded good, but helping these girls would be more difficult than ever now.

"You won't regret this, trust me," Tilly said.

I know I had a sour look on my face. Tilly ignored me.

"The girls have exercise class now, why don't you join them?" she said, like I was on some cruise vacation choosing my leisure activity for the afternoon.

I shook my head no.

"Come on, NaTasha, I have to meet with Red anyway, and I'm pretty sure they are playing your favorite today, volleyball."

I wanted to follow Tilly into Red's office to make sure she wouldn't find out my secret. Red had promised confidentiality, but who knew with this group. I did love volleyball, though, and the last thing I wanted was to make Tilly suspicious.

"Which way do I go?" I asked her.

"Shaunda will show you," Tilly said, waving over a tall, light-skinned girl. The girl had long dark hair and stood a foot taller than Tilly and me. And she was beautiful. Her hazel eyes were slightly slanted and her cheeks showed signs of the tiniest dimples when she smiled. Shaunda had to be some kind of supermodel. She smiled her perfect smile and kissed Tilly on the cheek.

"I think you girls will have a good time together," Tilly said. "You already have a lot in common. For starters you both love that ball game. Let me know who wins."

Tilly waved and swung her hips dramatically in the direction of Red's office. Shaunda and I laughed and headed in the opposite direction.

"So, NaTasha, how long are you in for?" Shaunda asked me as we walked down a quiet hallway. The artwork of leaves and tree branches on the walls resembled those in a doctor's office waiting room. I looked at her like she was crazy. "You're new, right? Well, what was your sentence?"

There was no way I could have possibly looked like one of these criminals. How could this girl think I was here because I had to be?

"Actually, I'm just visiting for a couple of weeks," I told her. Now it was her turn to return the crazy look. "Really, no sentence, no crime, just visiting and here to help out if I can."

"Right," she said. "Well, let's go."

It didn't sound like she believed me, but she didn't ask again, either. We turned the corner at the end of the hallway and pushed open a set of double doors that led to a gym.

The gym walls were painted a light purple, with a long row of bleachers lining one wall. The room was small and stuffy, like the walls were slowly caving in on us. A single tattered volleyball net separated the gym floor space, which we ducked under to join the other players.

One bag of uniforms lay up for grabs near the locker room doors. I wasn't surprised to find Quiana and Rochelle in the front, choosing their uniforms first and tossing the rest aside. Shaunda grabbed hers, and I was thankful to get one at all.

"I'll show you where to change," Shaunda said, leading me in the direction of the locker room. It turned out to be more like a large closet with a few sinks and toilets. Shaunda unlocked a locker far away from the others and told me to put my things inside.

"I was never good about trusting people," she said, making space for my things, "but if Tilly says you're okay, then you must be."

"So, what else do the girls do here besides volleyball and group sessions?" I asked her, putting on my T-shirt and shorts.

Shaunda pulled the striped uniform shirt over her head and it reached just above her pant line. She tugged at the shirt in discomfort and looked over to see if I was watching.

I unhooked Tilly's pearls and hid them in the corner of the locker. Wearing the pearls was like my shield of protection. It made me feel stronger, but on the court they'd only be in the way.

"Well, some girls are here for safekeeping," she said, answering me. "Some are here by order of the court. We do arts 'n' crafts, too. It's like an all-American day camp in here."

"Yeah, I can see that. I'm having tons of fun already," I said sarcastically.

"I can tell," Shaunda laughed and closed the locker. "Oh . . . and just so you know, hiding your goods in these lockers isn't going to make a bit a difference. If someone wants your stuff, they'll find a way to take it. I learned that the hard way."

I was embarrassed for trying to hide Tilly's bracelet. I had hoped Shaunda hadn't even noticed. I followed her out of the room and joined the other girls. They were all dressed and ready to play.

"Ladies, let's get going."

A black woman with more rolls than the Pillsbury Doughboy blew into a whistle and waved everyone over. She wore her hair in small dark curls, fresh from a roller set, without combing them through. The curls were lined like pastries in a store window display.

I stood next to Shaunda and waited for the lady with the whistle to give us more instructions.

"That's Anne West, but we call her Coach," Shaunda whispered to me while we waited. "She's all about good nutrition and healthy living. Ironic, huh?"

Coach West barely looked like she could climb a flight of stairs let alone practice sports. She reached into a cart of volleyballs and began handing balls out to the girls.

"Find a partner, ladies, and let's start passing around," she called. She took a deep breath and blew into her whistle hard like she was stopping an NBA game for a foul shot. After, she looked a little winded.

"Oh, and just a heads-up, she's whistle happy," Shaunda said, catching a ball from the coach. "You'll probably have a headache before you leave. Last month, she even wore the whistle during our Ping-Pong games."

"Hey, Coach, we have a new girl," Shaunda called to her. "This is NaTasha."

I waved and Coach came bustling over. She shook my hand vigorously and called an unhappy looking Quiana to join us. Quiana glared at me but didn't speak.

"Quiana, this is NaTasha, can you pair up and show her some of the techniques we've learned?" If only Coach knew our history, she would have asked anyone else in this room to help me out.

Quiana smirked in my direction, probably enjoying seeing me look like a charity case.

"I can't, Coach," she answered after looking me up and down. "Monique just asked me for help with her serve and you know I'm the best server you got. I'm sure they play some mean volleyball out in the suburbs anyway."

Well, I wasn't the strongest girl around, but I sure wasn't the weakling Quiana saw. I took the ball Coach West held out. Quiana smiled and walked back over to Monique. Those two would have a good laugh at my expense, I was sure of it.

"It's okay, I don't need her help," I said.

"Coach, my partner isn't here today. I can hit around with NaTasha," Shaunda said, coming to my rescue once again. "I think she knows how to play already anyway."

"Thanks," I mouthed to Shaunda, who set the ball in my direction. I returned it with ease and we quickly found a rhythm. The number of balls flying past my head was dizzying. Between the whirl of the balls and the sea of faces, the gym looked like a big bag of trail mix. So many shades of brown and orange it made me a little light-headed.

For a leisure activity, Coach seemed pretty serious about technique and the rules of the game. She weaved slowly between the flying balls, giving pointers and demonstrating the right way to hit.

I interlocked my fingers and stretched out my arms to wait for a pass from my partner. We hit back and forth for a few minutes before either one of us said a word. I listened intently to the sound of the balls slamming onto the court; the boom sounded almost like a horrible thunderstorm was brewing.

Shaunda was focused, apparently in some personal contest to see how many passes we could complete in under a minute. Sweat started beading up on my face and it already dripped from hers. I suddenly wondered about this overachieving, helpful girl who I was partnered with.

"So, thanks for helping me earlier," I shouted. "Don't take this the wrong way, but it doesn't seem like you need to be here."

"Thanks, I guess, but when I first got here, I was really messed up," she told me, releasing a small breath in between each word. "I'm out of here next week, but it took a lot of work to get to this point. You actually remind me of myself when I first arrived."

My blood rushed and I could feel my heartbeat speed up a little.

"What do you mean?" I asked her, more offended than I probably should have been. We kept the ball moving while we talked. I was glad for the distraction. Had we been in a quiet group session, I might have broken down and started crying. I hit the ball too hard by accident and it soared over Shaunda's head. I wiped my forehead and knelt down to catch my breath while she ran to retrieve the ball where it had landed, close to Quiana and Monique.

I heard a few giggles and looked to see if Quiana was doing the butt again. But she just looked at me disapprovingly. I was getting tired of that look.

"I used to hate everything about myself," Shaunda said when she returned. She hit the ball and we found a slow and steady rhythm again. I watched her graceful body movements and her strong, confident strokes and wondered how this beautiful girl could hate anything about herself. "I didn't look into mirrors for years. I was scared of what stared back at me. And I didn't like what I saw."

Shaunda wasn't in my group this morning. And I sure didn't tell her my secret. I glanced over at Quiana. She *did* have a big mouth. Maybe she had spread the word already. Or maybe Quiana and Shaunda were playing some trick on me. The girls were probably trying to find out as much as they could to laugh about me later. Or, set me up in another trap. What if I had said too much already?

It was strange and terrifying to hear my own thoughts about myself coming from Shaunda. But there was also something comforting about listening to her story, even if she was setting me up.

"I used to wear long-sleeved shirts and pants because I messed up my skin so bad," she said. "I would take baths in bleach, thinking it would change what I looked like. One day my mother caught me and took me to see a counselor about it. Being here helped, too. I could share my story with other girls who really understood me."

I hadn't noticed that I had stopped the ball and was standing with it underneath my arm.

"But weren't you scared to let anyone know what you were feeling?" I asked. As soon as I asked, I looked around to make sure no one was listening in on our conversation.

"Of course I was scared," she said. "Bleaching your skin isn't something you go around broadcasting, but holding on to my secret and trying to deal with my issues all alone was so painful and exhausting, it was nice to finally let people help me."

I thought about my group this morning. Susan and Rochelle had shared without reservation or concern that anyone would make fun of them. And no one did. Not even Quiana.

"You get to a point where what others think of you doesn't matter as much," she said, holding her hands out for the ball. "It's just easier to let it go."

A few of the girls started clapping and screaming on the other side of the court. Shaunda and I both turned to see what was going on. Monique had spiked the ball perfectly and was getting praise from the other girls and even from Coach.

"Hey, you still worried about what Quiana said to you?" Shaunda asked, while the other girls celebrated.

"A little," I told her. "She really hates me."

"Really, don't worry about it," she said, "she'll get to know you and everything will be fine. People are always scared and intimidated of what they don't understand."

I nodded to her and we started passing the ball again. After a few minutes, Coach West waddled over to us and blew her whistle. All the girls in the room looked over in our direction.

I felt my cheeks burning and my head started to throb a little, like I was pulling into the final stretch of a marathon on a hot summer day, when all eyes were waiting for me to hit the finish line. Coach West clapped and put her hands out, waiting for me to toss the ball her way.

I scanned all the eyes and wanted to cry. I wanted to finish first but I didn't want anyone to hold it against me. I didn't have to make friends, but I didn't want the girls to hate me, either. I found Quiana standing in the middle of the group, smirking. She didn't yell anything or make jokes; she just waited patiently for me to make a wrong move, trip, or lose my footing or something.

"NaTasha, let's go," Coach West said and clapped again loudly, rattling my thoughts. I threw the ball quickly and almost nailed her in the stomach.

"I want these two to demonstrate for you," Coach told the others, recovering from the catch. "Some of you aren't getting it. The key to winning matches is great form. You could learn something from these two."

Shaunda smiled proudly. I tried to think of a way to get out of this display. "Coach, maybe Quiana and Monique can show you . . . anyway, I'm not very good."

"NaTasha, I saw what you two did, and I asked you two to show me, so let's go," she answered a little impatiently, tossing the ball to Shaunda.

I shrugged in Quiana's direction to show her I'd tried. She put a finger in her mouth like she was gagging herself.

Shaunda rotated her shoulders back a few times and stretched her neck muscles, like she was preparing for a real match. She tossed the ball my way and we found a rhythm. I missed two sets from her, but the coach seemed happy.

"Do you see how NaTasha's arms are straight all the way through?" Coach yelled. "That's exactly what I want, girls."

I wanted to stop and dig a hole right in my spot on the court. I knew this praise from Coach couldn't be good. Everyone went back to passing around, with Coach going from group to group giving improvement suggestions. At the end of practice, Coach blew her whistle.

"Okay, ladies, divide yourselves, please, into two groups," she said.

The girls parted like the Red Sea. I didn't know which side to stand on. Even Shaunda had disappeared from my sight, so I was on my own.

Quiana passed by me on her way to the opposite side of the net and rolled her eyes. I wiped my sweaty forehead and tried to tuck my hair behind my ears. I looked around at the girls on both sides of the net. On my left side, the girls had light skin and long, flowing hair. I thought about Heather and Stephanie back home. Across the net on my right side, the girls had dark skin, and cornrows like Tilly's in their hair. Everyone in the gym looked at me.

"NaTasha, choose a side please," the coach said.

I looked at both groups, found Quiana on one team, and so chose the other.

"Take a good look, ladies," Coach West started. "Those standing on your side of the gym will be your team the next time we play. Now look at the ladies across the court. These are the young women you will be competing against."

The girls had divided themselves by race. If I had been given time to think about it, maybe I would have chosen differently. Maybe not, but either way, I was on the wrong side.

I felt sick. The eggs I ate with Tilly were swirling around in my stomach. Coach dismissed us and I left to find my clothes. The other girls moved just as quickly as I did, almost like they were trying to catch up. Quiana and Monique ran by first and brushed my right shoulder. I looked over and attempted a smile.

"Sellout." Quiana spat it at me like the word was dirt in her mouth.

I looked to Shaunda for help, but she turned her back and walked quickly toward the locker room. I held in my tears and got dressed more quickly than I ever had in my life.

Tilly was talking to Red when I made it to Red's office.

"We're almost done here, NaTasha," Red said. "I'm glad you came in when you did because you actually may be a big help to us next week. How would you like to help us plan our recognition ceremony?"

Apparently, these girls got certificates of achievement for surviving this program without killing one another. One girl would be chosen to give a speech of encouragement in front of parents and friends. After toasting with punch and cookies, everyone went home. Piece of cake.

What I really wanted instead of this prison sentence was to go back to Tilly's place and relax and never come back here again. That was it—no sharing, no planning, and no toasting.

For the next few days I could curl up with a good book until Tilly returned home. When I felt lonely I could sit on the stoop with Khalik and play cards or go order more food from Amir. He could give me long tours around the neighborhood during his lunch breaks.

Tilly and Red waited quietly for me to answer.

"Sure, why not," I said.

Not like I really had a choice anyway. Tilly would find some way to convince me, and if I sat around Tilly's place, I'd end up looking like the pampered brat everyone at Amber's Place thought I was.

"Excellent," Red responded quickly, clapping her hands together. "I'm so happy."

"Wait, what will I actually be doing?" I asked, like it really mattered. "Am I planning the whole thing on my own? Is someone going to help me?"

"We'll talk more about it tomorrow," Red said, "and maybe I'll assign a few girls to work with you."

And maybe it would be safer if *I* suggested someone to help me instead.

Tilly and I got on a downtown-bound train. I pushed my way through the crowd to find Tilly a seat and I stood above her.

"How was volleyball?" she asked.

"It was interesting, Tilly," I told her.

"Anything exciting?" she asked. "Did Shaunda take care of you?"

"We don't really play a real match until later this week, but Shaunda passed around with me a bit," I said.

I skipped the part about Shaunda being in cahoots with Quiana to ruin me. I skipped the part about my secret, too. Not a good idea in public where Tilly wouldn't think twice about embarrassing me.

When we walked up to Tilly's apartment building, Khalik and Rex were playing cards out on the stoop.

"Hey, Ms. Tilly, what's the word?" Rex asked.

"Just another day, Rex. How about you?"

"You know me, I'm making it," he said.

"Good, you take care now," Tilly told him. "Hey, Khalik, how's your mother?"

"She's good, Ms. Tilly," Khalik answered.

"Good, well you tell her I said hello and make sure you come up for pie sometime."

"Yes, Ms. Tilly."

Tilly headed up to start dinner.

"Tash, you want to play?" Khalik had turned all the way around in the wooden fold-up chair to face me. Rex stole a peek at his cards and I laughed.

"No thanks, guys, it's been a long day," I told them.

"Maybe next time," Khalik said.

"Yeah, maybe," I said. I thought about my smart plan to hang with them for the rest of my stay. I couldn't spend two weeks on the stoop. There wasn't even a place for me to sit. My cell rang. I waved to Khalik and Rex and picked up the call.

"Hey, Heather," I said. "How's the party planning going?"

"Oh, well, I could use your help coming up with ideas," she said nonchalantly, like working closely with Matt Billings was just as normal as eating lunch every day. "Got any?"

"Actually," I told her, "I can't help you. I'm planning my own party here. Amir may help me out, too."

"Who's Amir?" she asked. "I thought you liked some guy named Khalik."

"Oh, I didn't tell you about Amir?" I asked. "He's just this other guy who lives here."

"I knew you'd forget about me," Heather said in her whiny voice. "You've met *two* boys and you didn't even tell me. And you're throwing a party without me? You should come home, I miss you. I could even talk to Marcia if you want me to."

I hadn't even thought about ballet in what felt like forever. I certainly hadn't missed it.

"No, thanks," I told her. "Actually, I've decided to stay here a little longer than a week. You know, now that I have the party to plan and everything."

"What? I knew it!" Heather squealed. "You're changing. You haven't even been gone that long and I don't even know you anymore. Tash, you swore you wouldn't forget about me. And now you're staying longer, I bet there's more you're not even telling me, right?"

I started telling her about the girls, Amir, and even Rex. I almost told her about my secret. I didn't intend to hide things from Heather. But she wouldn't understand even if I tried to explain.

"Heather, are you still there?" I asked, thinking the line went dead.

"I'm here. I just didn't know you were miserable there," she said. "Amber's Place sounds so horrible. Why would Tilly put you through all that torture? Why would she bring you around people like that?"

"I don't know," I told her. "It's scary here, but not so bad. It's not like I have to live here forever or anything."

"If it's so scary, why don't you just come home now?" she asked, a little more forcefully this time. "Just call your mom and tell her to come and get you. We could go back to our normal lives. We could go shopping. We could both go to Matt's party together."

"It isn't that simple," I said, although there was nowhere else I'd rather be than in Matt's living room dancing to Coldplay and sneaking Coors Lights from his parents' bar.

"Of course it is," she said. "I could help you. We could call her on three-way right now. You could be home by the end of the week."

"My parents and Tilly are expecting me to stick this out," I reminded her. "Remember, my *new experiences*?" I had to admit, though, the thought of going back home was tempting.

"But they have you spending your day in a jail with girls who are nothing like you," she complained. "Why is that a new experience you need? I don't get it, Tash."

I thought about Shaunda and Susan.

"It isn't jail, Heather," I told her, "but I know what you

mean. I'll be home soon, you'll see, and everything will go back to normal."

"Yeah, we'll see," she said. "Well, I have to go. Stephanie and I are going to find party outfits later. I wish you were here, too."

That hurt. I went away for less than a week and my best friend had already replaced me with the girl who hated me the most. All of a sudden, home wasn't looking too great now, either. What did Heather expect . . . all three of us to hold hands skipping down the street when I got back?

"I hope you guys have fun," I told her, lying through my teeth.

"It isn't the same without you, Tash," she said.

"Clearly."

I THOUGHT ABOUT leaving Harlem all night long. Heather had been right. I could be home in Adams Park in a matter of hours with one phone call. I put my cell out of reach, but I eyed Tilly's gold rotary phone. It was the shape of an elephant. I touched one of the tusks and debated whether or not to make the call.

Tilly would get over it and Amber's Place would go back to business as usual with or without me. Red could find someone else to plan their recognition ceremony. I didn't have problems like those girls and I certainly couldn't help them. So what if I hated what I looked like, a lot of girls did. Who cared what those losers thought about me anyway?

But even if I did go back now, Heather had moved on without me. She was talking to Matt on the phone and taking trips to the mall with Stephanie. The thought of shopping with Stephanie was worse than dealing with the girls at Amber's Place.

I let go of the phone and slipped Tilly's pearls onto my wrist. One more day wouldn't kill me. If I made it through without incident, then maybe I'd stay. I could at least do one more day.

But what if I couldn't? I needed to tell Red to find someone else just in case. My heart wasn't in it and that wouldn't be right.

In the morning, I headed to her office first thing to let her know to look for someone else.

There was a handwritten note taped to her office door with my name on it that said,

NaTasha, come on in when you get here so we can discuss more about our recognition ceremony. You've made me so happy that you are going to help Amber's Place with such a special day. We really appreciate your support!

So I pushed the door open to Red's office and slammed into something.

"Hey, what the hell are you doing?" Monique hissed at me.

She fell back a little, but couldn't steady the books in her arms. They scattered around us on the carpet. She looked first at the mess and then at me.

"Of course it's you," she said. "You just can't get it right, can you?"

"Look, Monique, I'm really sorry, I was just coming to talk to Red," I said.

"Do I look like her?" she asked me with more than a little sarcasm. If I squinted, maybe they could be distant cousins.

"I actually didn't know you were here," I said, bending down to help her with the books. She kicked them out of my way before I could reach them. "What are you doing in here anyway? Did you get a note from Red, too?"

"Forget it, bitch," she said. "Red ain't here."

She pulled a thick manila folder from Red's desk and put it on top of her pile of books. I looked away quickly when she caught me watching her.

"I'm really sorry, Monique, I didn't mean to hit you with the door," I told her. I held the door open for her to pass by me.

She brushed my shoulder hard on the way out. "You better stay out of my way if you know what's good for you."

Quiana and Rochelle walked up just as she was leaving. Perfect timing.

"Stealing from boss lady already, Sellout?" Quiana asked.

I waited for Monique to give some sort of explanation. She stood quietly and all three of the girls looked at me.

"What are you talking about?" I asked her, feeling all of a sudden like maybe I shouldn't have been in Red's office while she wasn't there. I felt my face getting hot. "No . . . I was just . . . no . . . I wanted to talk to Red."

The girls laughed hysterically like I was a stand-up comedian telling them a joke.

"Looks like we finally found out why you're really here," Quiana kept on. "You pretend you're better than us black girls, pretend you're an innocent white girl from the suburbs, when really you're just a low-life thief."

She slapped five with Rochelle but she may as well have slapped me instead.

"I don't know, Quiana, do you think we should tell Red about this?" Rochelle asked sweetly. "She ain't going be too happy at all about this little wannabe white girl breaking into her office and snooping around with Monique. I think we should tell her, what about you?"

This was bad. Red probably expected this from Monique, but Tilly would have a heart attack if I got mixed up in something, even if she believed me. Red didn't know me from Alice Junkie on the street. Quiana and Rochelle started walking down the hallway. Monique and I were left to clean up the mess.

"I don't steal," I said, closing the office door.

Monique glared at me and stood directly in front of me, almost close enough for our noses to touch. Every time I moved back, Monique stepped closer until I was pressed up against the door. Claustrophobia didn't describe the lack of air I was getting at that moment.

"It was an accident," I whispered, trying to convince her everything was fine. If Red had met me here, I wouldn't be in this mess. Wherever she was, she had no idea I was about to get pummeled outside her office. "Please, let's just drop this and go to group."

"So, what were you doing in here anyway?" she hissed. "You come barging in first thing, with your ugly pressed hair and swinging the hips you wish you had and talking all proper and shit. You think you're all that. But you ain't all that. You're a sellout. I'm getting sick of seeing your ugly face. Why don't you just go back to where you came from, because we don't want you around here no more."

What had I done in my lifetime to do deserve this? Quiana and Rochelle had slowed down and turned to listen to Monique berate me.

"You," she said, coming even closer to me, "have been trying to pick a fight with me since you got here. So let's go ahead and do this."

Quiana and Rochelle had walked back toward us and now stood facing me like a firing squad. Quiana folded her arms across her chest.

"I wasn't picking any fights," I said.

Monique shoved me hard, and my purse fell from my shoulder. The lack of space between us made my whole body hot.

I continued, "Like I already told you, I was just trying to talk to Red about the recognition ceremony, that's it. I don't care why you were in the office and I won't tell Red anything, I promise."

"Hey, Monique," Rochelle said, "the white girl thinks you're a dummy *and* a thief." She turned to me. "You think Monique didn't hear you the first time? You think you can take us, *Sellout?*"

Clearly there was some miscommunication going on.

"What?" I asked. I'd never been in a fistfight in my life. I certainly didn't want to fight these girls. "Look, I don't know what you're talking about. I won't say anything about you being in there and she doesn't have to know any of this ever happened."

"Oh, isn't that sweet, Monique," Quiana said, smirking. "The sellout is trying to save your ass again. What would you ever do without her?"

Rochelle laughed and shoved her friend playfully, which only made Monique more upset. Quiana shoved Monique then, too, who slammed her hand into my chest. I fell back into Red's office door and tried to catch my breath.

I swallowed the acid taste in my throat and, so as not to further embarrass myself, pushed Monique back off of me. But Monique was too fast and caught my arm.

"Look at these, girls," she said, holding up my wrist with Tilly's pearls hanging there like a prize. "I bet these are real special to our little princess, huh?"

Tilly was going to kill me. I grabbed Monique's arm to get her off of the bracelet. She yanked me sideways and pulled the bracelet right off. The pearls spilled onto the floor like raindrops. They rolled and bounced in every direction. I dropped to my knees and tried to gather them before they scattered too far, but the girls were faster and had a good time kicking them out of my way.

"Look, girls. Now the sellout needs *our* help," Monique said. "Should we help out?"

They hated me. My hair, my skin, my body, my voice, they hated everything I hated about myself. I was just like them after all, because I hated me, too.

The laughs engulfed me like flames. I picked up every pearl that I could find through my haze of snot and tears.

Quiana had a smile on her face I'd never forget, a wide one that sparkled like she had just gotten away with murder.

I turned and started to walk away.

"Monique, this girl still thinks she's better than you," Quiana told her friend. "She's walking away and doesn't even think she needs to apologize. What are you gonna do about it?"

I turned around. Monique was furious. I pleaded with her with my eyes to let this go and allow me to help her make it right.

"Who the hell are you anyway? It's obvious you don't belong nowhere around here," Monique said. I paused to think about a right response to her challenge. "Hello?"

I opened my mouth to answer, but my throat was dry and my voice cracked terribly. I cleared my throat and tried again.

"I can't help who I am," I said quietly.

"You hear that, Mo?" Quiana asked. "Now she wants us to feel sorry for her."

It was true, even I sounded pathetic to me. I waited until they all stopped laughing and tried again. "And I didn't choose to come here."

"Yeah, well, NaTasha, we're *so* glad you did. I can tell we're all going to be great friends," Quiana said, rolling her eyes toward Monique.

"Fine," I said, surprising myself. As soon as I said it, I

wished I hadn't. The summer was too long to face these girls as my enemies.

"Hah, you a tough girl now, NaTasha?" Quiana asked. "Monique, I think she thinks she can beat you. What do you say about that?"

Monique didn't say anything.

She grabbed my hair. I swung my body to get her off me, but she was too strong. Soon, I could feel her nails against my cheek and then a pain shooting down my back. I pushed her hard. Tilly's pearls exploded from my grip again. The girls stood laughing at me before rushing off down the hallway toward the main meeting room, leaving me on my knees.

There was no way I was sitting with any of these girls for group time. They could share without me and laugh about me the whole time if they wanted to. I picked up as many pearls as I could find and ducked into the bathroom.

I set the beads in a paper towel. I patted my cheeks, which were still blazing hot. The fresh inch-long scratch on my left cheek from Monique's fingernails burned. Maybe now Tilly and Red would think twice about recruiting me to be the one trying to help these girls. Looks like I needed just as much help as they did, if not more.

I pulled out my makeup from my purse to see if I could somehow cover up the scratch before I got on the train. I didn't need to walk around broadcasting the fact that I'd just been beat up.

The blush powder burned as soon as it touched my skin but I spread it anyway. I covered every inch, from the dark circles under my eyes to the tips of my ears. The girl staring back at me in the mirror made me sad, and a little sick to my stomach. My hair was frizzy and looked windblown, as if I'd just walked inside from a storm. I smoothed it down as best I could.

When I was all done up, I counted the number of remaining beads. More than half of them were missing. My hands shook wildly but I carefully tucked the remaining pearls into my handbag.

I wrote Tilly a note on a paper towel and slipped it under Red's door before heading for the exit. I stayed clear of the main room.

The train was packed. Didn't anyone in this city vacation? No matter where I turned, millions of people crawled around like ants, busy little workers finding food and supplies to return to their anthills. And I was the only one who noticed. Old men pushed past women like they didn't even exist. Kids my age took seats and let elderly people with canes stand above them on the trains and didn't think anything of it. Street vendors yelled obscenities loudly like they were the same as morning prayers, and no one blinked an eye. There was only one person who would understand all of this.

"Heather, call me when you get this," I said, leaving a message on her cell. "I had a terrible day and I really need to talk to you."

Heather never turned her phone off. I pictured her sitting at Matt's place talking themes for his party, which made me more upset. I hoped she'd get back to me soon. When I got to

Tilly's neighborhood, I headed right for her front stoop. Rex and Khalik were there playing cards. I sat down next to Khalik. He nodded while he passed out his playing cards but didn't speak. Rex picked up each card Khalik handed him and examined them closely.

"Man, why don't you wait until you got them all?" Khalik asked.

"Nah, I got to make sure you ain't trying to cheat me," Rex said, winking at me.

"Have I ever cheated you before, old man?" Khalik asked, still flinging the cards between them. Rex scooped up each one.

"That don't mean jack and you know it," Rex told him.

When the cards were all in place, Khalik turned to me, looked me up and down, and shook his head.

"Damn, you look a mess. What happened to you?" he asked me.

I shook my head and looked down into my lap. They didn't need to know what went down at Amber's Place. They wouldn't be able to do anything about it anyway, so what was the point? Khalik turned back to the game when he figured out that I wasn't talking.

I watched them throw the cards down and argue back and forth for a while. Every so often one of them would steal a glance at me, but they let me just sit and watch. The more I tried not to think about the fight, the more upset I got. I had held it inside for as long as I could, but eventually a tear escaped, falling down my cheek.

"You know what I think?" Rex asked to no one in particular. No one answered him, but he kept talking anyway. "The human race is going down the toilet. We have no leadership, no sense of community anymore, and people are just afraid. They are afraid to reach out to one another. Rather than helping one another, we're hurting one another because of what we don't know and what we don't understand."

"Hmm . . . I hear that," Khalik said, throwing a king onto a teetering pile of cards.

I wiped the tear from my cheek, but another fell in its place. Khalik handed me a tissue from his pocket but stayed focused on the game. He paused and looked like he wanted to say something, but he let me be. I was glad.

"Sometimes on the street, people look at me like I'm some kind of disease," Rex continued, "like I'm not good enough to walk on the same sidewalks as they do."

I'd never thought about how hard Rex's life must be. He always looked content to me. His shopping cart was filled to the brim with torn blankets and plastic bags full of canned goods. A pair of sneakers was thrown over the top, almost holding everything in place to avoid an avalanche of his belongings. Living on the street must be rough, but I'd never heard him complain or even talk about it.

"It don't seem fair, do it, Ms. NaTasha?" Rex said, finally looking up at me. I wasn't quite sure what he wanted me to say, but I nodded my head in agreement. "But you know how I learned to deal with it? I just held my head high no matter what. And I also learned that for every jerk that passes by, there are two or three good ones that come by soon enough. You kids need to learn that."

I kept nodding because he was right. I wondered if I could find even a handful of nice people at Amber's Place to make up for the bad ones I'd run into so far. I thought about Shaunda.

When they finished the game, the guys leaned back with their elbows on the stairs next to me. We sat like that until the sun changed positions in the sky. The streets started to fill with more people. Soon Tilly would be back and I knew she'd have a million and five questions for me to answer. She must have been shocked to discover I wasn't in the building with her all day.

We watched her neighbors go by, everyone headed home for dinner. A group of guys around my age joked with a taxi driver, who didn't look pleased to have to take the group anywhere. He reluctantly unlocked the doors and drove off with them down the street. I could also see Amir. He was unloading boxes from a delivery truck. I watched him work for a while until he caught me staring. I looked away quickly but waved when I could feel he was waiting for me to look back at him again.

"Looks like you got an admirer, young lady," Rex said, with a smile on his face.

"Whatever," Khalik said, "that dude ain't nobody. Look at him, he works in that funny outfit and he ain't got no peoples to hang out with."

"That's what I'm talking about right there, son," Rex said. "You don't know nothing about that cat, but you talking bad about him. You should go meet him and then see what you think. You two might have a lot to talk about."

"I ain't got shit to say to that dude," Khalik said, standing. "I'll catch you all later. Keep your head up, Tash."

Khalik moved quickly and was already through the door by the time I turned around to say good-bye. I wondered why he was suddenly in such a rush. Rex must have thought the same thing and shrugged his shoulders like he didn't know why, either.

"What are you all doing out here?" Tilly asked, as she crossed the street toward us. She was carrying two grocery bags at her side. I ran to take them from her with the cut side of my face turned away, and then walked behind her. It was only a matter of time before she discovered I'd been in a fight, but later was definitely better than sooner in my case. "What happened to you, girl? I was worried."

"I just needed a break, that's all," I told her, which was half of the truth. I did need a break from all that madness. Tilly didn't need to know I was running away to hide from those terrors at Amber's Place. "Sorry I worried you."

"I got your note, so I knew you weren't lying somewhere hurt, but you should have come to find me," she said, squeezing her hips through the front door. "Evening, Rex, you want a plate?"

"No, thanks, Ms. Tilly, I'm headed to the church tonight," he answered, moving toward his cart. "You know they got my favorite meat loaf tonight."

"Alright then, Rex, we'll catch you later," Tilly said, starting to close the door behind us. We waved to Rex as he wheeled away down the sidewalk.

When we got inside Tilly's apartment, Tilly set her purse down and went straight to the kitchen. She smiled and reached for two place settings, each decorated with a different pattern of painted apples and vines. When we sat down to eat a short while later, she didn't waste any time.

"So, are you going to tell me about the day, or am I gonna have to hear it from someone else?" Tilly asked. "What's the matter, girl, tell me about it."

I put a forkful of salad in my mouth and tried not to look her in the eye.

The collection of pearls I'd picked up off the ground was burning a hole in my pocketbook. Tilly had a way of finding everything out, without asking. I knew she better hear it from me.

I swallowed hard and looked her in the eye. She wiped her mouth with a napkin.

"Tilly, I broke the bracelet," I told her. I pulled the loose pearls out of my purse and placed them on the table between us. She finished chewing what was in her mouth before she said anything. She eyed each pearl, almost like she was counting.

"I'm sorry, Tilly," I said.

"How did this happen, NaTasha?" she asked quietly. "You know I don't own much and I trusted you to keep up with my jewelry."

I felt horrible. I couldn't look at her anymore. I thought I saw a tear forming around her eyes. If only I'd knocked first before rushing into Red's office or just kept my mouth shut, none of this would have ever happened.

"I fell." First I broke her jewelry and then I lied. It *was* a fall, after Monique knocked me down, but it was still lying. "I fell coming out of the bathroom today. The pearls got caught in the door and I went down like a bowling pin."

I'd have to find some way of repaying Tilly for the broken pearl bracelet.

"Oh. Well, did you hurt yourself?" she asked, looking at the scraped skin on my face. I couldn't believe what I was doing. I'd never lied to Tilly ever before. I leaned in and showed her my cheek, where Monique had grabbed me. She traced her fingers across my face and watched me carefully. I pulled away quickly and put more lettuce in my mouth.

"You fell, huh?" she said, taking another spoonful of the greens.

I nodded yes, but couldn't bring myself to look at her anymore. Our eyes didn't meet, but I could feel her gaze like I could feel a fork scraping across my teeth.

"Did anything else interesting happen?" she asked.

"Nope," I said.

"Nothing?" she prodded. "You're sure?"

I thought about all the bad things these girls had said to me so far. It seemed like Amber's Place had been a part of my life forever and not just a few days.

"Tilly, why do these girls hate me so much?" I asked before I could think better of it. I really wanted to know. Quiana was so angry and I couldn't figure out why her anger was directed toward me.

"Someone said they hated you?" she asked, sounding surprised. She put her fork down onto her plate.

"Yeah, in the gym yesterday," I told her. "I guess I stood with the wrong group of people. But I didn't understand what was going on."

"It sounds to me like you stood with the right people and didn't get yourself wrapped up in silliness," Tilly said.

I put my fork down, too, and pushed the plate away from me a little. Tilly sighed and kept talking. Something about her tone and facial expression told me she'd had this very same conversation with someone else before.

"There's a difference between being proud and being ignorant," she said. "Don't you choose ignorance, you hear me, girl? Those girls believe because you are different that you can't still be just like them. And we know that isn't true. People fear what they don't know."

When Tilly gave words of wisdom, I listened. She stood up after that, leaving some untouched food, and started clearing the dishes. Tilly had gotten most of the dishes from the table and turned on the hot water to start washing. I walked up behind her and hugged her tight.

"I tried to be nice to those girls and they don't want anything to do with me," I told her. "They are so different from the girls at home. I really miss my friends. I miss the way things were."

"I know, baby, I know," she said. I wanted to ask more and find out what she knew, but she sighed again and I could tell she was getting tired. "It'll get better in time, you'll see."

I trusted her and desperately wanted to believe her, but it was hard to. We cleared and washed until every dish was returned to its proper place in Tilly's cabinets.

"Tilly, I'm really sorry about your bracelet, but don't worry, I'll replace it," I told her.

"I know you're sorry, baby," she said. "I'm not worried about those jewels. I'm glad you're okay. And you know you can talk to me about what really happened whenever you're ready."

I opened my mouth to protest, but she closed her bedroom door before any more lies could come out of my mouth.

I knew Heather would call me back after she got my message, so I wasn't shocked when the phone rang. She was already talking when I picked up the line.

"Hello?" I asked. "Heather, who are you talking to?"

Two voices giggled back at me. There was someone else on the line, which annoyed me. I was in no mood to be toyed with, not after the day I'd had. Heather should have been able to recognize that in my voice when I had left her the message earlier.

"Tash, you have to, like, guess who it is. You'll never believe it!" Heather said, sounding like a three-year-old on Christmas Eve waiting to open a room full of presents. "Go ahead and guess."

If she only knew how *not* in the mood I was for this.

"You have three seconds, Heather, and then I'm hanging up," I said as sternly as I could. The two of them giggled again. "I wanted to talk to you about my day."

Heather didn't answer at all. I could tell by her silence that I'd hurt her feelings. Well, she'd get over it.

"It's me, NaTasha. It's Stephanie." Stephanie said this like I was supposed to be excited to hear her voice. "How's the big city treating you? I decided that I'd forgive you. Actually, Heather convinced me. So we can all be friends, okay?"

What in the world was my best friend doing on the phone with my biggest enemy? I must have a tattoo on my forehead that read TORTURE ME or something because I just couldn't win.

"Stephanie, what's up?" I asked flatly.

Heather jumped in before Stephanie could answer. "What's got you in, like, such a sour mood, Tash?" she asked.

"Maybe it's the fact that I wanted to talk to my best friend about the rotten day I've had and she calls with the one person who hates me most in Adams Park," I said. Yeah, it was rude and I didn't care.

"Look, I already told you what to do about your situation at that crazy place, Tash," she said, like she was talking to a stranger on a telemarketing call. "If you don't like it, then come home already. No one's forcing you to stay there. But we didn't call to talk about that. We have some exciting news for you."

We didn't call? I didn't know what had gotten into Heather, but I sure hoped she didn't seriously think I'd be excited to hear any news from the girl *we* used to hate.

"What's the news, Heather?" I asked reluctantly.

"Get this . . . we got the *same* haircuts today," she screamed into my ear. "They're, like, totally the same. Stephanie's hair stylist was awesome and she gave us a great new look."

"Wonderful," I said, holding the phone about a foot away from my ear. This could not be happening. I'd been replaced, by a party, a new outfit, and a pair of shears.

"I know! They look great. You could get one, too, when you come back," she said, waiting for my reaction. I didn't have one. "How cool would that be? Then we'll all look like sisters!"

I would look as much like those two as an elephant does a zebra.

"Well, not *exactly* alike, Heather," Stephanie said, throwing her little laugh into the mix again. She was starting to sound like long fingernails dragging across a chalkboard. "I'm sure my stylist could try, but NaTasha wouldn't look *exactly* like us."

"Of course she would," Heather said, sounding confused. "I, like, so don't get it."

"Why do you sound like that, Heather?" I asked her. The high shrill sound was working my nerves.

"What are you talking about?" she asked.

"So, how long exactly are you going to be gone, NaTasha?" Stephanie asked, interrupting again.

That was it. No more Ms. Semi-nice Guy. This conversation was over.

"Okay, it's been great catching up, but I have more important things to worry about than cutting my hair," I told them. "Heather, maybe I'll talk to you later when you're not so busy."

"NaTasha, wait, we have another surprise . . ." she started.

I hung up the phone, feeling like crap, which was starting to become all too familiar a feeling these days. I flopped onto the sofa without undressing or showering. Cleaning up right then wouldn't have made my deep state of funk go away anyway.

CHAPTER NINE

I WOKE UP feeling like something had shifted inside of me. Despite the nasty fight and the disturbing phone call from home, I felt stronger somehow. And I knew I couldn't go home.

Rex was right. For every one jerk, there had to be at least two more nice people to balance the world out. I had met the mean ones already at Amber's Place, so today the nice people had to make a comeback.

Quiana, Rochelle, and Monique had already done their damage. There was nothing left for them to do to me. If I ran away, they would win. I may not be able to compete physically, but they weren't going to make me run away, too. I would plan the best recognition ceremony they had ever seen. I couldn't disappoint Red or Tilly anymore. I had already told Red I'd help and already lied to Tilly, so I owed them.

Tilly was silent all the way to the train station. She eyed me a few times, though, and every time I turned my face away so I wouldn't have to talk about what happened by Red's office. Tilly had let me avoid the subject so far, but I knew it was only a matter of time before the story was out.

When we stepped onto the train, a young guy got up and offered Tilly his seat. I stood directly in front of her, waiting for her to look up. She didn't. Right then I knew Tilly wasn't very happy with me.

"I wonder what's going on at Amber's Place today," I said in Tilly's direction. When Tilly didn't respond my heart sunk. I couldn't have Tilly not on my side. Not with so many people already against me. The other passengers looked around to see who I could be talking to. I didn't like everyone's eyes on me like I was some crazy person, but I was desperate for Tilly to talk to me. "We have that volleyball match today. I hope we win."

Now I was having a full conversation with myself. The couple sitting to my left stood and found seats near the other end of the car, so I sat down. A few others eyed the empty seat next to me, but no one moved. I didn't blame them. I wouldn't want to sit next to a crazy girl who talked to herself, either.

"I sure hope we win or at least come close," I said, more loudly than before. "I was thinking of wearing my famous ballet scarf bun for the big game, what do you think?"

Tilly glanced over and grinned a little bit. It worked. She always liked when I made her laugh. I reached for her hand and she took it. Her hands felt rough, but just around the edges, like she washed dishes but applied the right amount of her cocoa butter lotion.

"Let me tell you a story," she said softly.

I leaned closer to Tilly and listened to her over the roar of the train.

"When I was your age, I walked into a similar situation as you, NaTasha. I was the new girl at school, struggling to find myself, struggling to find a place where I fit in, to be accepted for just being me. I searched for a long time, because, unlike you, I didn't get that kind of support at home. I looked to my friends at school and some kids who shouldn't have been my friends. Most of them were just looking to take advantage and have a little fun with the new girl."

Tilly paused for a minute. I held my breath, hoping she wouldn't change her mind about talking to me. I wanted to hear anything from her at this point. She had never told me much about her childhood, just that her high school years in the Bronx were the worst.

"A girl approached me in the hallway one of my first days at that school and asked me if I wanted to sit with her and her friends during lunch. I didn't know anyone else, so I said yes. I didn't understand until later how bad of a decision it was to align myself with this group of girls. I just wanted to fit in and have friends."

Tilly seemed to be in some kind of trance, as if the girls were sitting right in front of her and she was telling them her side of the story. She continued softly.

"Once I got to the table, the girls created a list of tasks that I had to complete in order to gain their full friendship. Each task was a little harder than the other, and a little more illegal than the one before it. But I did every last one of them. I wanted to be friends with them so badly. When the list was completed, I thought I was done. But I was wrong."

Tilly's voice started to crack and she squeezed my hand hard.

"I knew those girls weren't worth my time, but I let it continue anyway, just so I wasn't alone. A few nights later, I got invited to a slumber party. The girls took turns yelling questions in my face and then spitting at me when the answers weren't right. The next day at school they apologized and told me they were only having fun with me. I forgave them right away, but the next night it was more of the same, except they wanted to see how much pain I could handle. One girl would pull my hair and see how long it took me to scream. I came home with so many patches of my hair missing that my mother thought I'd been in a fight. And now that I think about it, I was in a fight. Those girls punched at me and kicked at me like I was a robber trying to take away all of their money. It was almost two weeks before I spoke to them again, but they convinced me, somehow, that things would be different. This time I followed them on the train to a part of New York I'd never been to. We were supposed to be touring a new neighborhood together. I turned my back for a second and they were gone. I had to find my own way home. Eventually, I learned to start making decisions for myself again. These girls were not my friends and as soon as I realized that, I was better off."

The tears were flowing from my eyes. A little boy sitting across the train car handed us tissues from his backpack. I reached for the tissues and tried to clean myself up. Tilly went through some pain, too. I guess we all had to go through something.

I held Tilly's arm to help her off the train and followed her through the turnstile and out onto the street.

"Wow, Tilly, I didn't know you went through anything like that," I told her. "Why didn't you ever tell me any of this?"

"Tash, all the girls at Amber's Place have a story, including you and me. This building we meet in is named for a girl who couldn't handle the pain of her abuser anymore. Amber Chambers ended up taking her own life. But that's what the girls are learning here: We are stronger than any pain that may come into our lives. That's what Amber's Place is all about. Baby, there is going to be struggle in your life that you can't possibly prepare yourself for, but let me tell you from experience, if you run from it, it'll just follow you to another place in your life. You have to learn to face your fears."

We stood in front of Amber's Place and Tilly wrapped me in a big hug. My heart beat uncontrollably at the thought of walking through those doors. But, with Tilly's encouragement, I was ready to face Monique again.

"I really hope you decide to stay and plan this recognition ceremony, but I understand if you can't," she said, looking at me as if she were waiting for my answer on the spot.

Tilly squeezed my hand again and walked toward the entrance. Before she got too far away, I called out to her. "I'll do my best," I said. Tilly nodded and I followed her inside.

Group time went by uneventfully. The girls stared at me and I stared right back. My life at home was so easy compared to what I was facing here. I had no idea how to help these girls, when I needed some myself. But I had to stay and figure it out. When Red dismissed us, I walked toward the gym, carrying Rex's words and Tilly's advice along with me.

"Whose side you gonna be on today, Sellout?"

Quiana started in on me as soon as I walked through the gym doors. Coach was late so I was on my own, sort of like Tilly was on her first few days of school. The image of Tilly's hair being pulled had stuck with me. Nothing Quiana said to me now could affect me the way she wanted. I pictured her in Tilly's story. Quiana was the one pulling at Tilly's hair. My face grew hotter and hotter every time she opened her mouth. But I was not going to let her win.

"Maybe if we help you, you'll know which side you belong on," Quiana said.

She and her girls had me surrounded. Every girl in the gym looked our way, but no one moved. Quiana had everyone under her spell. Even Shaunda shook her head and looked the other way. I guess she figured she had rescued me enough already.

Quiana and Rochelle surrounded me. Rochelle stood so close behind me I could smell her cheap perfume.

"Leave me alone, Quiana," I told her, my skin starting to crawl. "You don't bother me."

"Oh, yes I do," she laughed. "If I didn't, your face wouldn't be all red and your body wouldn't shake like a little leaf."

The girls laughed. I just stared right through them. Pretended they weren't even there.

"I'm shaking because I can't wait to beat your team out there today," I said.

"Yeah, whatever, Sellout," Quiana said now. "We'll see just how good you play today. Rochelle is the best player here."

Their team nodded and slapped hands with one another. Rochelle was a little too close for comfort. If I stepped back at all, I'd be lying in her lap.

"Yeah, I guess we will see," I said too confidently.

Rochelle had about three inches on me and her width was the size of a quarterback. Clearly, she could take me out with one swing, but I pretended not to care.

The girls laughed and started to shove one another playfully, intentionally bumping me around. The picture of Tilly in a circle being shoved around just like me popped into my head and I clenched my fists tightly.

"Cut it out," I told them, trying to push my way out of their trap.

They laughed and kept shoving. I saw Tilly back on the train with her head down. I pushed them back as hard as I could and knocked Quiana down. All the laughter stopped at once.

Rochelle grabbed on to a chunk of my hair and yanked my head back. I could see Quiana struggling to get onto her feet quickly. Everything was silent now. Every eye was on us.

"You bitch," Rochelle screamed. "You're really gonna get it now."

"You just don't know when to quit do you, Sellout?" Quiana yelled.

The gym doors flung open and Coach West came barreling in, the whistle blowing loudly between her lips.

"We'll settle this later," Quiana whispered. "That's a promise."

I joined my team but stayed clear of Shaunda, who waved me over. I was just as angry at her as at Quiana at the moment. Where had she been a few minutes ago?

"Okay, ladies, let's get changed and ready to play," Coach said. "We have a match to settle. When you get back, grab a ball and separate into your teams."

I pulled on my gym shorts and T-shirt and laced up my tennis shoes as fast as I could. This was my chance to shine out on the volleyball court.

Back in the gym I joined my team and prayed for a miracle. Two girls next to me had taken the time to braid their shoelaces into a pretty pattern. They reminded me of Heather and Stephanie and their stupid matching haircuts. Shaunda stood behind me and ran her fingers through her hair over and over again. This would be a long match. None of the girls on my team seemed to care whether we won or lost.

I wondered if anyone besides Quiana and Rochelle noticed how out of place I was on my team. There was a clear separation of color. I was on the team of girls with white skin and long hair. I stood out like a sore thumb. Quiana and her gang smirked at me from the other side of the court.

"NaTasha, is everything okay?" Coach asked, before we started. She must have seen that I was surrounded by trouble as she flew into the gym. I glanced over at Quiana, who stared at me with an all-too-eager look in her eyes.

"Everything's fine," I said.

"This is going to be fun," Rochelle said, directly across the net from me.

Coach blew her whistle and the match began. Soon all I could hear were the grunts after a hit, the squealing of shoes skidding across the floor, and the whistling of the ball slamming into the net. Rochelle was good. She made every set that was sent her way. Every time I raised both hands ready to receive a ball over the net, she reached higher to connect with the ball.

We rotated every point until my turn to serve came. I took position outside the line and held the ball outstretched in my left hand.

"Choke, bitch," Quiana pretended to cough into her hand. The girls on her squad laughed.

I served while they were still laughing at Quiana and scored a point for our team. My team gathered together in the center of the court and cheered. It wasn't game point yet, but it felt good.

"That was the last one, Sellout," Rochelle yelled to me.

"Okay, girls, let's keep up a positive playing atmosphere," Coach yelled, behind her clipboard. Positive playing atmosphere . . . How could she be so oblivious?

Rochelle had new fire in her eyes. I served again and this

time Quiana's team was more than ready. We passed back and forth a few times, and then Rochelle hit a line drive at my head.

"Miss it, Sellout," Quiana yelled again from her spot on the court.

I swung too soon and the ball smacked me in the nose before I could slam it back over the net. I felt my face explode like an overfilled dam.

My team surrounded me. Through their muscled legs, I could still see the huddle of girls across the floor congratulating Rochelle for taking me out of the game. Coach decided the amount of blood coming from my nose was enough to send me to the nurse. I wanted back in.

I was completely covered by the time I reached Gracie, a volunteer nurse at Amber's Place.

"*Dios mío!* What happened?" she asked, sounding alarmed.

"Oh, just a volleyball accident," I told her. My nose felt like it wasn't there anymore. My whole face throbbed and hurt even worse when Gracie applied alcohol on it with a gauze pad. I felt around to see if my bones were still there. Gracie pushed my hands aside. Her gloves were covered with my blood.

I wondered if Tilly had ever had a bloody face from the girls who tormented her. It was hard picturing my grandmother with a bloody face, or playing volleyball for that matter. Somehow, Tilly had survived and learned how to handle herself with people. And now she always knew the right things to say and the right way to act. I had to learn, too. Gracie wiped my face clean and put a bandage over my nose, but it felt like my whole head was wrapped like a mummy.

"You want me to call Tilly for you?" Gracie asked.

Although I wanted Tilly, I didn't want to disturb her or make her worry. I sure didn't want Quiana and Rochelle to think they'd gotten the best of me.

"No, thanks, Gracie, I'll be okay," I said. I sounded like I had the worst sinus infection of my life. "I'm going back to the gym."

Gracie gave me an unsure look, like she didn't want to send me back to the wolves, but I didn't give her much choice. I hugged her quickly and walked out of her office and back toward the gym.

When I got there, the girls got a good laugh at my bandaged nose. The game was still going. Rochelle's team had the lead. Coach came over to see how I was doing.

"I'm ready to play, Coach. You can put me in," I told her. I was ready for Rochelle this time. I wouldn't take my eyes off of her. This was my only chance to get back at her. Coach stopped me before I made it onto the court.

"I don't think so, NaTasha," she said. "Why don't you just sit back and relax for the rest of the game. I don't want any more accidents for today."

The look on Rochelle's face said it all. They had won. It didn't matter what the score was. I had been defeated.

"Yeah, Sellout, why don't you just sit back and relax," Quiana said. "By the way, I like your bandage. It matches."

"What's your problem anyway?" I asked her.

Quiana dropped the ball and walked straight toward me. My insides started to rumble. Coach blew her whistle, but no one listened.

"What did you say, Sellout?" she asked.

She stepped toe-to-toe with me. My heart dropped. If I played my cards right, she wouldn't hit me in the nose.

"Why do you call me that?" I asked, trying to steady my voice. Tiny beads of sweat started to form on my top lip and around my forehead. I didn't dare move to wipe.

"Because you are a sellout, stupid," she said angrily. "You have no idea who you are. You think you're a white girl and you think you're better than the rest of us."

She was glaring at me like I had tried to hurt her or something.

"No, I am not and no, I do not," I shot back. "You don't know anything about me."

"Relax, girls," Coach yelled. "Let's get back to the match."

Even though I wanted to confront Quiana, I could feel the tears welling up. I looked up at the rectangular fluorescent lights hanging from the ceiling so the tears would stay in place. When I looked back at Quiana, I could tell she wasn't going to let this go. Her teeth were clenched, along with her fists, and her temples pulsed. She looked like a bull ready to charge.

"You talk like a white girl, you dress like a white girl, and you even wear your hair like a white girl," she pointed out. "And you mean to tell me you don't think you're a white girl? You're more stupid than I thought."

Tilly popped into my head again.

"I'm not stupid, Quiana," I said.

Coach blew the whistle loudly. Quiana and I both ignored the loud warning.

"Yeah, you are, Sellout," she said.

"No, I'm not," I told her, my voice rising to match her own.

"Yeah, you definitely are," she said, laughing now. I crossed my arms over my chest and ignored the steady stream of loud whistles coming from Coach. She wedged herself in between Quiana and me. Every eye was on us to see how we were going to settle our score.

"Well, I can't imagine what you're fighting about with a girl who hasn't been here long enough to pick a fight with anyone, Quiana," Coach said. "You must want to sit out the rest of the game."

"Coach, she's a rat, and you know how I feel about that," Quiana said confidently. "You mess with me or my girls and I'm gonna give you what you ask for."

She said it to Coach, but it was really meant for me. I had no idea what Quiana was talking about. Me? Messing with *her* friends? As if I would dare mess with any of them.

"But I didn't do anything, Quiana," I said.

"My girl Monique says otherwise," she shouted back, "and she's not here right now because of you."

Rochelle was standing behind Quiana, glaring at me. What had Monique told them? I wasn't a rat. I hadn't said anything about Monique to anyone. My heartbeat jumped into my stomach. I had to bend over a little in order to steady my breathing.

"Okay, I've heard enough," Coach said, pointing her finger at Quiana. "You're out. Sit down and watch the game, because that's all you're going to be doing for a while. NaTasha, you feel well enough to play again? It looks like it is more dangerous right now for you off the court than on."

I nodded and followed my team back into the game.

COACH WANTED TO see me in Red's office after the match was over. I dressed in record time to beat the locker room traffic — wild girls who liked to bully me in secluded places.

"NaTasha, come on in," Red called to me. Coach was sitting in one of the comfy chairs near the door.

"Hey, Coach. Hey, Red," I said, leaving the door open behind me. "What's up?"

"I just wanted to check in with you to see how your first couple of days have gone here," Red said, moving her computer keyboard off of her lap and back onto her desk.

They leaned forward and looked intently at me, like they really cared about what I had to say. I wasn't so sure. Coach had now witnessed my torture firsthand. Maybe this was her way of reaching out to me. But I wasn't ready for her help just yet.

"Oh, thanks, but everything is fine," I told them.

"Are you sure there isn't anything you want to share with us?" Red asked. She opened a manila folder, similar to the one Monique was stealing earlier. "It can stay between us if that makes you feel more comfortable."

Red wanted me to rat on Monique. That would just give Quiana and her gang real reason to rip me to shreds. I pled the fifth.

"Nope, everything is fine," I told Red, even as she eyed all of the bumps and bruises that had appeared on me in the past few days. "The match got a little rough today, that's all."

Coach looked at me then and cleared her throat. She and I hadn't had a whole lot of time together, but she understood my look of desperation, the one pleading with her to keep quiet.

"The match was a rough one for her, Red," Coach answered after a long pause. "But NaTasha is a great player. You should come and watch the girls play sometime soon."

Red seemed unsure that everything really was okay, but promised she'd come by to see for herself when she got the chance.

"Okay, then, NaTasha, are you still on board to help with the reception ceremony?" she asked, changing the subject.

She handed me a list of guidelines and procedures to read over when I got home. I took the paper from her and perused it while she kept talking.

"So, it has come to my attention someone was in my office yesterday morning," Red said. "A few girls walking by saw the light on."

I sat quietly and let her keep talking.

"So, that list is not final until I find out what happened," Red continued. "We might have one less girl for the ceremony, but I'll let you know when I know."

"Okay, sounds good," I said.

My heart jumped into my throat and started doing jumping jacks. I reviewed the list in my hands. There was a question mark near Monique's name.

"Too bad and a lot of work down the drain," Red added. "I guess she wasn't as ready to move on as I thought. I've asked her to come in and speak with us regarding what happened yesterday morning."

There was a knock on the door and, almost as if on cue, Monique stepped through the doorway. That was my sign to exit.

"Okay, well, I'll look through this and get back to you tomorrow," I said, not waiting for a dismissal. Coach West was already standing, though, blocking my escape. She closed the door to my freedom and all I could do was stare.

"Actually, NaTasha, one of the girls said they saw you exiting the office yesterday morning as well, so I'd like you to stay," Red said.

Monique looked right at me, probably praying I wouldn't say anything. No way was I going down for something she did on her own. Red motioned for me to sit next to Coach and I did.

"Red, I wasn't even in here yesterday morning," Monique said smugly, before she was asked anything. I sat and tried to pretend I wasn't present for this interrogation. I picked at my nail polish.

"No one said you were, Monique," Red said. "So, you didn't stop in at all?"

"Nope," Monique lied, glancing at me. I stared at her but kept my mouth shut.

"NaTasha?" Red asked. I reluctantly turned to look at her. "*You* weren't in here, were you?"

All eyes turned to me. I couldn't believe Red was even asking me. Monique folded her arms across her chest and smiled.

"I came to talk to you," I said quietly. "You weren't here, but I got your note to come in. I assumed you wanted to see me about the recognition ceremony."

"Of course, that's right, NaTasha," Red said, shaking her head. "I forgot I asked you to stop by. I apologize."

Monique pretended to be hurt. "Where's my apology? I wasn't even involved."

"No one was accusing you, Monique," Red said. "I was just asking a question."

Her voice was calm and steady. If someone broke into my space, I would have been livid. I thought about the story Tilly told me about her childhood. I wondered if she had ever been falsely accused.

"NaTasha, I do have one more question," Red said. "Was there anyone else here with you yesterday morning?"

The tension in the room was heavy. I could tell this wasn't the first meeting for Monique about stealing. Coach sat with both arms folded and Red flipped through her pages full of meeting notes. Monique sat quietly but firmly, ready to pounce at any sign of opposition. She glared at me.

"NaTasha?" Red asked.

I could easily get back at her for yelling at me, for scratching my face, and for breaking Tilly's bracelet. She had to pay for what she'd done to me. It was my turn to look smug. I folded my arms and smiled at her. For the first time she looked nervous. I didn't take my eyes off of Monique.

"No, no one was here with me."

They all looked shocked, especially Monique. Her face softened a little.

"Are you sure about that, NaTasha?" Coach asked.

"Yeah, I'm sure," I told them.

"Red, can I go now?" Monique asked.

"Monique, I just want to remind you about my rules," Red said. "You have been here a long time and I would hate to have to see you extend that unnecessarily."

I expected Monique to come back with some curt, smart-alecky remark. I chipped away the last piece of polish from my thumbnail and snuck a peek at her. But this definitely wasn't the same girl who had tried to pound my face in earlier.

"Okay, girls, you can go, unless you have something else to add," Red said.

I expected Monique to smile or to acknowledge I'd just helped her out of trouble. But, I got nothing. She wouldn't even look at me. This must have been what Rex meant by the good guys making a comeback.

"Actually, Red, I'm sorry I didn't mention this earlier," I started. Monique froze and looked me squarely in the eye then. "I am going to need a little help organizing the ceremony, especially since I'm new here, and have never actually been to one."

I stared at Monique as I spoke. She bent down and pretended to tie a shoelace.

"Not a bad idea," Red said. "Monique, since you're here, please assist NaTasha with whatever she needs. We'll meet again soon to touch base."

Monique stared at me with her mouth wide open. I thought she would pass out then or break into violent rage, slamming things around the office. Planning anything with me was the last thing she wanted. But, she had no choice.

"Do I have to?" Monique asked. I thought I spotted a smile on Coach's face.

"We could go back to our previous conversation if you prefer," Red said. Monique stayed quiet and shook her head no. She gathered her things quietly. "Good, then. I think you two will make a great team. You can include others if you need to. Let me know as soon as you can what supplies you will need."

I followed Monique out of the office. She went one way and I went the other. At that moment I wondered if I'd done the right thing.

CHAPTER ELEVEN

SHAUNDA MUST HAVE seen me heading for the ladies' room, because she was hot on my heels just as I shut myself into a stall. I could hear her shuffling around in her bag, pretending she really needed to be in there, but I ignored her.

When I came back out she looked at me sheepishly. "I wanted to say sorry to you for this morning on the court," she said. I stared at her blankly, forcing her to recall her betrayal. She lowered her head a little and began. "I should have defended you. I'm sorry, NaTasha."

I had to face those girls on my own. Some friend she was. My real friends would never have treated me like that. I thought of Heather. I would have had to pull her off Quiana. Well, maybe not, but she wouldn't have let me fight alone. Shaunda had left me out in a pack of wolves to survive on my own.

I didn't say anything. While I waited, I poured out the contents of my purse and decided to touch up my hair. I wet a paper towel and wiped my face clean, careful not to ruin the bandage. My face felt rough and it throbbed from the scratches

I had endured earlier. I pulled out my comb and raked it through my hair a few times.

"It's just that I have been trying to steer clear of those girls for so long now," Shaunda continued. "They used to torture me so badly. I'm finally ready to move on with my life and I just want to leave here peacefully without them bothering me anymore."

I glanced at her in the mirror next to me. I rolled gloss on my lips and handed it to her when I saw her admiring it.

"It's MAC's new stuff, sparkles a little, too," I told her, completely ignoring her apology.

"Thanks," she said, almost in a whisper.

"No problem," I said, taking back my gloss. She put her pointer finger between her lips and dabbed lightly.

"So, what is your history with those girls?" I asked. Somehow I knew the story wasn't going to be pleasant. Shaunda took a deep breath and turned to look at me. I hadn't forgiven her yet. She'd left me hanging like a dirty washcloth on the court. I pulled the comb through my hair several times again slowly. She turned back away from me to dab her eyes dry. I watched her open her own purse and take out a jar of skin bleach and use the paper towel to add a new coat to her cheeks, forehead, nose, and chin.

"What are you doing?" I asked her. "Why are you using that? How long have you been doing that to your skin? That stuff is really not good for you."

I tried to take the bleach away, but she held it out of my reach.

"I know what it does for me, NaTasha," she said. "It makes me forget who I am, and reminds me who I want to be. I have never fit in my whole life. Not with white girls, not with black girls, not with Hispanic girls, not with Asian girls, no one."

I looked at her clear, light skin with model bone structure and wondered if she had one of those body identity crisis disorders they talked about on *Oprah*.

"I know it sounds crazy," she said. "All my counselors and family members have told me so. But, I still hate what I see in the mirror."

She started to cry. I put my arm around her shoulders but as much as I wanted to encourage her, I just couldn't. I knew exactly what she was talking about. Her pain was the same as mine.

"Did Quiana tease you about your skin color?" I asked, hoping to calm her down.

Shaunda turned her whole body toward the sink bowl and dry heaved a few times.

"I'm sorry, Shaunda, I didn't mean to upset you," I told her.

"Look at this," she said, holding her arms out in front of me.

She rolled her sleeves up. Her skin was layered and discolored. There were small burns on the back of her arms.

"Quiana teased me about these marks," she started. "When I figured out I couldn't fit in, I started bleaching."

Tilly was right. Everyone had a story.

"I didn't like my skin," Shaunda continued, "so I tried to change it. I thought I could keep that to myself until Quiana found out. She thought it was disrespectful to her personally because of her own dark skin. She found any opportunity to hurt me and then she did."

I handed her a paper towel to wipe her tears.

"She used to call me 'Scar' whenever I walked into a room to make the other girls laugh at me," she continued, "but then she got worse. She would yell things out while Red was talking or in the middle of our group. Only a few people knew she was referring to me, but I started having nightmares thinking about how she would embarrass me next. I had to see a psychiatrist. I couldn't sleep, let alone explain what was happening to me."

I rubbed her back in small circles. I wasn't angry anymore. Shaunda had been through worse with Quiana and her gang.

"My parents tried to help." She kept talking. "But they didn't understand. My mom is white and my dad is black. Quiana is the reason I'm still here. Red doesn't think I'm stable enough to leave. All I really need is to get away from this place and I'd be fine. I've felt like a prisoner here with that girl."

"I wonder what makes Quiana that way," I asked. Shaunda snapped her head toward me in shock.

"You haven't heard?" she asked me. "I thought Tilly would have warned you."

I thought Tilly told me everything.

"She was molested by her uncle for years," she said in a whisper. "Her mother is still on drugs. Amber's Place is Quiana's only *real* home. Red is the one who has taken care of her, but Quiana is just mad at the world. She hates anyone who has had a more privileged life, which is about everyone and anyone."

"So, what changed?" I asked. "Why are you ready to leave now? What made you strong enough to get past all of her torture?"

"One day I decided the teasing wouldn't get any better unless I accepted who I was and was happy about it," she said. "It's a process. I'm not all the way there, but I'm trying. I'm not hurting myself anymore and that's what I'm working on."

Shaunda looked at me, and I looked down at the small bleach bottle in her purse.

"Like I said, it's a process," she said, "and when a new girl shows up to take the attention away from me, Quiana leaves me alone for a while."

I had rescued Shaunda.

"Just be careful of those girls, NaTasha," Shaunda said. "I know you aren't here for long, but don't let them get into your head and affect you the way I've let them do to me."

"Oh, I'm not worried about them," I told her confidently. I wanted to tell her all about the meeting we'd just had with Red and Coach, but there wasn't time. Tilly had to be waiting for me by now. "They can't possibly hurt me anymore."

"Just be careful, okay?" she asked.

"Sure, but I have a feeling things will be different now," I told her on my way out of the restroom. I had to go and face Tilly, with my bandaged nose, scratches, and all. It was time to tell her the truth about what I'd let these girls do to me.

"HEY, MISS LADY, where you headed?" Rex yelled when he saw me coming.

Tilly had given me a new grocery list as soon as we stepped off the train. She headed inside to start on dinner and I walked as slowly as I could to avoid seeing Amir at the meat counter.

First the beans, now my bandaged nose. Amir was going to think I was a train wreck. My nose had stopped bleeding, though no amount of foundation powder could cover this mess. "Hey, Rex, how are you today?" I asked him. I hoped Rex was having a better day than I was.

Rex was leaning against the wall of the bodega, right underneath a Help Wanted sign that hung in the window. I wondered if Rex had noticed the sign or if the owner would hire him if he ever applied for the job. I ducked under the sign next to Rex to hide just in case Amir was around.

"Oh, I'm hanging in there, NaTasha," Rex answered. "And how might you be this fine afternoon?"

"I'm alright, I guess," I told him. I pointed to my bandage and he frowned. "I could be worse, I guess."

"Damn right it could be worse," he said, looking around him. I immediately felt like unlacing my sneakers and sticking one inside my big fat mouth. He smiled and set his Need Money and Work sign down.

It was a warm day, but he still looked cold, wrapped in several layers of tattered clothing and a heavy snow coat on top of all the layers. I broke a sweat just looking at him. I wondered how he survived on these streets. I wanted to ask about a shelter or a church or somewhere he could sleep indoors. I didn't. He'd been taking care of himself long before I had gotten here.

"I'm glad you're doing well, girl," he sang. "God is good, ain't He?"

"Yes, He is," I answered him.

At the bottom of his sign were the words GOD BLESS YOU.

I reached down and put my pocket change into the bucket next to his sign.

"You know Tilly would kick your butt if she saw you doing that," he said, smiling.

I held up a finger to my lips and smiled back at him. The roundest black woman I'd ever seen exited the bodega. She rolled her eyes at Rex and shook her curly fake hair in my direction.

"You know, he's been sitting in the same spot for years," she said snidely. "He could have bought a condo on Riverside Drive by now with all the money we give him. Rex, you should be ashamed of yourself."

"I'm just a vet trying to make it, Shirley," Rex said. Shirley had her hand poised like she didn't want to hear another word.

She moved toward the street and used the same hand to stop a speeding taxi, still eyeing Rex and me out of the corner of her eye as she squeezed herself into the backseat.

If it was me sitting on the street with a cup and a Need Money sign, I wondered if anyone would care.

"Wow, she seems nice," I said.

"Yeah, she's a real piece of work," Rex said, with a gruff laugh.

I didn't know how he was able to deal with it all. I get teased a few times and I'm ready to run home. I wondered if Rex had anyone he could to run away to.

"You better get back before Tilly comes looking for you," Rex said.

He was right. Tilly was probably rushing around the kitchen, waiting for me to return with the groceries, so I stood, debating whether to go inside.

"Hey, Rex, is there another store anywhere close?" I asked, pointing to my nose again. I peeked in the front window.

"Yeah, walk two blocks that way," Rex said, pointing down the street, "and you'll run right into it. Careful, though, their prices are high over there."

I walked down to the other store and grabbed a red grocery basket. As I walked through the store, I added to Tilly's list of items.

I paid for all the food and headed back for Tilly's apartment.

"Hey there, NaTasha," a voice called behind me. "How's your visit with Tilly going so far?"

I was already at the stoop of Tilly's building. I was nowhere near his meat counter, but I recognized Amir's voice right away. I froze in place, hoping some other girl named NaTasha was on the block at the same exact time that I was. Amir tapped me on the shoulder.

He looked amazing, even in the white butcher apron. He was supposed to be cutting meat behind the counter in the back of the store.

"NaTasha?" He walked around me so we were face-to-face.

"Huh? Oh . . . hey," I said, and smiled weakly. I put my hand in front of my face like I was trying not to spread germs. "How are you?"

"Good, except they have me pulling a double shift today," he said. "I'm working the front and the back."

That didn't explain why he was here, standing in front of me. There had to be some reason. I smiled at the thought and waited for him to point out the bruises or my bandage, but he didn't.

"Oh, that's too bad," I said, still staring.

"So, are you going inside or are you just going to hang around the doorway all night?" he asked. He still made no mention of my swollen face. What a great guy.

"Oh, I'm on my way upstairs," I said. "Tilly asked me to pick up a few things for her and I was already a few blocks away from here."

"That's cool," Amir said, eyeing me and the bandage. I don't think I could humiliate myself further in front of Amir if I tried. I would have to shop at the other store from now on. Amir gestured toward my face. "Is everything okay?"

"I've only been here a few days and already decided on a nose job," I said. We both laughed.

"How is Ms. Tilly?" he asked.

I pictured her cooking and humming in the kitchen. Pretty soon she'd be walking downstairs to find out what was taking me so long. The menu for the night was pot roast.

"She's fine, you want to come up?" I asked him. He pointed to his watch and shook his head. "Well, I'll tell her you asked about her."

"See you later?" Amir asked. He sounded hopeful.

"Okay," I said.

When I got back to Tilly's apartment, she was checking on a delicious-smelling roast. One hand was on her hip and the other was frantically seasoning the meat.

"It's about time. That boy better not be the reason you took so long," she said, huffing like she just finished a race. "I love him and all but you better watch yourself, girl."

"Tilly, please," I told her, setting down the bags quickly. "There was a long line at the checkout, that's all."

She slammed the cabinet shut and sucked her teeth. She wasn't buying it. I took the butter out and scooped a chunk into a pot to boil some rice.

Before long, Tilly had pot roast and green beans ready and waiting on the center of her table. My rice was a little overdone and I'd made enough for five people, but I set the bowl on the table.

"Anything exciting happen at the center today?" she asked, taking a bite. She already knew everything that went on. I didn't know why she even needed to ask.

"Not really," I said, waiting for her to beg.

"Really," she said, scraping some rice onto her fork with her fingers. "Nothing at all? You better stop playing with me, girl, and tell me what happened to you. I'm too old for the guessing games."

"Well, I got a bloody nose during the game and I had a meeting with Red, Monique, and Coach about a little misunderstanding," I said quickly. "But don't worry. We worked everything out together. Monique is going to help me plan the recognition ceremony."

"Really?" Tilly asked. "And how do you feel about that?"

"Oh, things are getting better with the girls," I told her, before biting into my food. "I'm sure everything will be fine now."

Tilly set her fork down slowly and tilted her head to the side. She looked confused and relieved at the same time.

"What, Tilly?" I asked her. "Really, things will be fine."

"Just watch your back," she said quietly, picking up her napkin to wipe her mouth. "I didn't put you in an easy situation and I certainly didn't put you here to get hurt. Just watch yourself and be careful. Don't ever forget that, okay?"

I didn't know everything about the girls at Amber's Place, but I was smart enough to know that nothing about my life back home would help me out in this situation.

"Don't worry, Tilly," I told her, "I've got everything under control."

"Alright," she said. She picked up her fork again to finish off the remaining rice and green beans on her plate. "So, what was the misunderstanding with Monique?"

"Someone thought she was in Red's office yesterday morning," I said. "It was all just a mix-up."

"A mix-up, huh?" Tilly asked.

"Yeah, a mix-up," I said. "We're supposed to meet tomorrow to start planning."

Tilly put her fork down again. To date, this was the slowest Tilly had ever cleared her plate. We'd been sitting for almost a half hour and she still had food left. I should have known she was really worried.

"Just be careful," Tilly said. "Monique may not even be able to talk to you tomorrow. You know it is visitor's day at the center. The girls can invite anyone they like to visit in place of their group time. Her bad-news boyfriend is scheduled to come. The guards warned me earlier today. Apparently, he ain't one to write home about."

I put my own fork down and put one hand over my grandma's. I hadn't seen her this worried in awhile, not since she caught a glimpse of my scarf bun during my recital.

"Don't worry, I'll be careful," I told her, just as my phone rang.

I left Tilly at the table and answered.

"Hey, NaTasha," Heather said sullenly.

"Hey, yourself," I said, wishing I had let the call go to voice mail.

There was a long awkward pause, as if a stranger were calling and we had no idea what to say next. The call didn't seem like one from my best friend in the world. The silence was unbearable.

"So, I have some great news," I said. "A few of the girls from the center are going to help me plan the recognition ceremony."

"You're planning what?" she asked quietly.

"Oh, they recognize the girls for completing the program at Amber's Place," I told her. "So, what's been up with you?"

Silence again. Most people who make a phone call to someone have something to say.

"Well, aren't you going to tell me about Stephanie and how you two are inseparable now and how the matching haircuts are so cute and how you're best friends with her now?"

I hadn't meant it to sound as pathetic and desperate as it came out, but that's exactly how I was feeling. And she should have already known that.

"Oh, wait, let me guess, Stephanie is on the phone again, right?" I accused.

"No, she's not, and, Tash, I just wanted to say I'm sorry," she answered. It hadn't been that long since she and I were sitting on my bed staring at the plastic stars on my bedroom ceiling together. "I never should have had Stephanie on that phone call. She really is trying to be friends now, so I thought we could give her a chance."

We? It was my turn to stay quiet.

"Did you hear me, NaTasha?"

"Well, I'll think about it," I said. More silence. I wanted to know exactly what the two of them had been up to, but she had just apologized, so I left it alone.

"It sounds like you're busy and starting to have a good time there," she said. "Are you homesick at all?"

I couldn't tell her how badly I wanted to be home with my best friend or how much it was killing me not to be able to go to Matt Billings's party. She wouldn't understand how terribly Quiana and Monique were treating me. I didn't want to explain how miserable I was, so I lied.

"Yeah, it's great," I said, "I even talked to Tilly about staying for the whole summer. The girls at Amber's Place really need my help and all, you understand."

If only she knew how far I was reaching to pull out that lie, she might never speak to me again. I didn't even know where it was coming from. I wasn't a person to lie, especially not to Heather.

"That's great," she said flatly. A tinge of anger and resentment swelled up in me.

"Okay, well, it's been great catching up," I said, rushing her off the phone. "Have fun at home and tell everyone I said hello."

"Okay, bye."

I hung up before she or I could lie any further.

I went back into the kitchen to help Tilly clean. Thankfully, she didn't ask me any questions about what she'd just overheard, which was good because I wanted to process what had just happened. Scrubbing the dishes and double drying them didn't seem to ease my mind, so I convinced Tilly to let me sit on the stoop for a while before turning in.

I wasn't the only one having trouble relaxing.

Khalik was sprawled across three steps. If I didn't know him better, I would have assumed he was another homeless guy napping on the stairs.

"What are you doing out?" he asked. "I thought all you goody-two-shoes types went to bed early on school nights?"

He laughed at his own joke and I smiled. If only he knew how badly I had just treated Heather, he wouldn't think I was so good at all.

"Good thing it's not a school night," I said, after trying to come up with a better comeback than that. "What about you? Why aren't you out harassing some innocent girls on the street?"

"'Cause it's too much fun to sit here and harass you," he said, winking at me.

I looked into the street and watched a kid driving an Escort slowly down the block. I had the urge to run next to the car just to see if I could beat him to the stoplight.

"So, what's up?" Khalik asked, rolling onto his side so he was facing me. "You look a little better without the bandage. I see the girls at Amber's Place are warming up to you already."

I shook my head, feeling like the tears would come if I opened my mouth at all. Khalik was full of jokes, and had a good laugh at my expense.

"Really, I was just playing earlier, I'm not here to harass you," he said, removing the pick from his hair. "You can tell me what's up."

What's up was I was confused, confused about Amber's

Place, confused about home, confused about me, confused about everything. How could I explain all that to him without sounding like a nut?

"I just got off the phone with my best friend," I said, quietly, hoping I wouldn't cry in front of him again. "And it didn't go well."

I glanced at him. He was listening and not laughing, so I kept going.

"I think she's replaced me already," I told him. "I haven't even been gone that long and I'm already replaced."

"That's messed up," he said.

He shook his head like he knew what I was talking about. He pulled himself up until he was sitting right next to me on the same step. I could smell the chocolate scent of his hair lotion and sniffed slightly to get more. It was nice of him to listen.

"All I wanted to do was tell her how things may have taken a better turn at the center today," I said, "I didn't even get to tell her about the girls and who I'd be working with. She wasn't really interested."

"So, what is going on up there?" he said. I could tell he was trying to change the subject to get my mind off of Heather. I let him. My head was starting to hurt a little anyway. "I think I know somebody that goes there."

"Who is it?" I asked.

"This chick named Monique," he said nonchalantly.

I looked at him to see if he was joking. He could tell I must have made some connection because I scrunched up my face and looked away immediately. He smiled slyly. It was an incredibly small world.

"How do you know her?" I asked.

"Long story," he said quickly. "Me and that girl used to date back in the day but she had mad issues, way too much to deal with. You meet her or something?"

"Something like that," I said, not wanting to get into it anymore that night.

"Well, just look out for her," he said, standing up and brushing off the back of his jeans. "She can be a piece of work. I'll catch you later."

He left me there to think about what a "piece of work" she had been already. My trip down to the stoop had turned out to be just as disturbing as my phone call. Khalik and Monique? Dating? Sleep was out of the question for sure.

CHAPTER THIRTEEN

IT WAS PERFORMANCE time again. I pulled on a black tutu over a black leotard and tied a black ribbon into my hair. Marcia waved us all over but skipped our normal warm-up routine. She said we needed to focus more on the proper ways to braid, so that's what we did, braided and rebraided our hair.

When all of our braids looked the same — mine with more scarf than hair — we marched to the stage in military precision and waited for the curtain to rise.

Small billows of smoke filled the stage floor and the curtain rose on cue. Hundreds of clowns applauded for us as we pirouetted onto the stage.

"What's going on?" I asked the dancer to my right. I couldn't picture her face or her name. She wore a pair of stockings covering her face, like she was hiding her identity. It was almost as if she had no face at all. She turned to me and smiled an eerie grin but kept dancing. I turned to Marcia on the side of the stage. She pulled on a clown mask of her own without looking in my direction.

"Marcia, what is happening here?" I whispered loudly. She didn't respond but clapped along with the other clowns. "Answer me, what is this?"

I spun in perfect time with the music. Apparently, the other dancers didn't think so. They formed a circle around me and pushed me around and around until everyone had a chance to shove me. I spun like I was on a Ferris wheel at a carnival. I looked for anyone who was familiar to me, anyone who could rescue me, but found no one.

"I don't want to do this anymore," I screamed over the music, waving my hands back and forth above my head. "Stop it, please stop it."

The dancers let me out of the circle and jumped into the audience, who roared approval at the show going on. I searched every face in the audience, one by one. Tilly or Mom must be out there somewhere. And where was Heather? We always danced the same numbers. I'd never been onstage without her.

I turned around and there she was.

Heather and Quiana wore matching red tutus and skipped across the stage hand in hand. They laughed loudly and pointed in my face.

"Are you kidding me?" I asked. "Heather, be careful, she's danger-ous. You have to stay away from her."

The pair kept dancing as if I weren't talking at all. More smoke billowed higher and higher into the air, making it harder for me to watch my best friend and my worst enemy, and easier for them to hide from me.

"Tag, you're it." Heather reached out and shoved me across the stage.

"Tag, you're still it, Sellout." Quiana shoved me even harder. I landed on the floor facedown. I stayed that way until I felt two pairs of strong arms dragging me back onto my feet.

Amir and Khalik carried me like a sack of potatoes and placed me on a pedestal to face all the clowns. The audience threw steaming hot combs and bottles of hair lotion at me at full force. I ducked and dodged as much as I could, but got hit several times. My nose started to bleed. Large welts started to appear on my skin and all I could do was stand and cry.

"Help me, please," I asked, reaching out for my friends.

The girls stood with their arms around one another's shoulders, while the boys stood guard next to me as if I were a prisoner about to be stoned by an angry mob.

Amir and Khalik arrested me for dancing in an illegal space and proceeded to take me to a jailhouse. Amir slapped high five with Khalik as they locked me into a cell.

I was behind bars, but I swayed along with the group as they skipped away.

"Tash, wake up! It's me. What are you carrying on about in here?" I could hear Tilly's voice in the distance and looked around my cell to see where she was. "Girl, you are drenched. You're gonna lay here and catch pneumonia."

I'd had a crazy dream or two in my lifetime, but my attack of the clowns took the cake. Tilly was standing over me, laughing.

"Girl, you were having some kind of dream last night," she said.

"Tilly, there were clowns and I was onstage again," I started telling her, while freeing myself from the tangled sheets. "The smoke was everywhere and Quiana was dancing with Heather. Even Amir and Khalik were there. They put me in a cell."

"You must have caught a chill in the night or something," she said, wiping my forehead dry. "That must mean you're in for a heck of a day."

"Yeah, that's what I'm afraid of," I said quietly.

Maybe the Amber's Place girls weren't going to have a change of heart as I had hoped after all.

When we walked into Amber's Place, I was still trying to convince Tilly about the clowns and the smoke. She had laughed at me the whole train ride.

"Alright, I'm headed to see Red," Tilly said. "Try and forget about that silly dream and have a good day."

She kissed my cheek and walked down the hall giggling.

I headed off in the direction of our group meeting room, where the visitors were gathering. I didn't want to miss the opportunity to learn more about these girls. I watched the security guards pat down a few rough-looking kids in oversize clothing.

I sat down to watch all of the girls with their visitors. Most girls invited a parent, some had invited a friend, and some had asked boyfriends to come. Red and Tilly walked around greeting everyone and reminding visitors of the rules.

The whole sight just made me even more homesick than I already was. Maybe I should have asked my parents to visit or even Heather. She was probably too busy gallivanting around town with Stephanie, her new BFF.

"Don't have anyone coming to see you, either, huh?" Quiana was stretched out across a couch behind me. I hadn't even noticed her there. She smirked, but kept watching the security guards like she was expecting someone.

I shook my head no when I realized she was actually talking to me. "You?"

"Not that it's any of your business, but no, my grandmother had to work," she said. "No one else gives a shit."

It wasn't so hard to believe. I wondered if her grandmother was actually working or if she was really just a figment of Quiana's imagination.

"That's too bad," I said, not knowing what else to say.

If it were anyone else, I would have offered to keep them company until the visitors left. With Quiana, it was probably best for us to stay on our respective couches. I didn't want to go home with any more black eyes if it wasn't absolutely necessary.

"Not really," she said coldly. "I get to watch all these other fools act like they care about each other."

She nodded her head in the direction of Monique and a grown man. Monique was holding yellow roses and her boyfriend had a box of chocolates open on the table next to them. Half the box was empty already. He probably ate them on the way.

Monique's boyfriend had to be at least ten years older than her. I thought I saw gray hairs peeking out of his Afro. She had her head tilted to the side and a silly grin on her face, like he was casting love spells on her. Quiana stuck her finger in her mouth and pretended to gag. I laughed.

"Well, maybe they really do care about each other," I offered. She looked at me with disgust on her face. I shrugged. "You never know, they could be in love."

"What do you know about it anyway?" she asked roughly. "He ain't no good and Monique knows it."

"They look happy together," I said cautiously.

"Yeah, well, you're wrong," she said, kicking her legs out in front of her.

"How do you know so much about them?" I asked.

Quiana faced me squarely with her elbows on her knees. She was either gearing up for a fight or getting comfortable to tell me a really long story. She looked back over at the happy couple again.

"It wasn't too long ago he was behind bars for hitting her," Quiana said. She sucked in her breath, like she had spilled a secret no one was ever supposed to find out.

"She called me up one night and said he came to her place trashed," Quiana continued. "She couldn't get him off of her, no matter how hard she fought him. I jumped on the train and got to her as fast as I could but he'd already knocked her out cold. She woke up in the hospital with more bruises than an old piece of fruit. Her momma didn't even recognize her. I showed her the birthmark on 'Nique's thigh and she about fell out, too. I stayed with her in the hospital for three days over him. And now look at her."

Every muscle in my body was tense, like I was watching a movie where the murderer was about to attack an unsuspecting victim.

Quiana had to be pulling my leg. I stared at her, but she glared at the "happy" couple with such intensity it was enough to blind a person. If it weren't for the small tears in the corners of her eyes, I would have called her a liar. I wouldn't have actually said it, of course, but I sure would have implied it.

"Damn, my allergies are acting up again," she said, reaching for a Kleenex.

I wasn't sure what the right thing to say was after a story like that. While deciding, I kept close watch on Gray Hairs. It was hard to believe this man was capable of hurting Monique. They looked so happy, both smiling and leaning into each other. How could Monique be that way with someone who had put her in a hospital?

"Why in the world would Red let someone like him in here after all that?" I asked Quiana, when she was done "clearing up her allergies."

She rolled her eyes first and then kicked her legs back onto the couch.

"She knows he's bad news, but really she don't know the whole story," she said. "Red likes to give *everyone* a second chance."

Quiana looked right at me when she said this, either telling me Red wasn't as smart as she appeared or Red had given her a second chance or two over the years. Curiosity nearly pushed me onto the couch next to her.

"So, is that how you're still here?" I asked, nearly whispering. She didn't answer. I was digging too much. "Do you feel like you have to protect Monique?"

"You ask too many damn questions, you know that, Sellout?" she snapped. I nodded my head yes, still waiting for the answer.

"Since you'll probably keep asking, she's helped me out before and that's how we roll," she said. "Now, bounce and go bother someone else."

I left, feeling like Quiana and I had made huge progress. We actually had a full conversation, without any punches thrown. There was potential there. But we had a long way to go. I smiled as I walked away.

Tilly and Red held a planning meeting for the recognition ceremony for all the girls after visiting hour was over. When I walked in they were seated close to one another, laughing about something Red was saying. I pulled up a chair next to Tilly.

Monique and Gray Hairs had said their good-byes, with Quiana watching them like a hawk. They both walked in the room a few minutes after me. I smiled at Quiana and moved my chair over to make room for hers next to me. She sucked her teeth and dragged her chair loudly across the floor away from me. Then Maria waddled in behind the others, holding her stomach, and sat down next to Red. The rest of the girls followed suit until we had a full circle.

Tilly reached over to put her arm around my shoulder and squeezed me a little.

"Okay, ladies, it's that time of year again," Red said. "A few of you are leaving us because you've proven over time that you are able to be productive members of society again and will no doubt be moving on to bigger and better things. NaTasha and Monique are working together to plan the recognition ceremony, so let's hear your ideas of what you would like them to be like."

"It's about damn time I get out of here," Quiana said, rolling her eyes to get the other girls wound up. It worked. She slapped high five with Rochelle, who folded her arms roughly across her chest. "I think we should get balloons, confetti, and all that."

"Let's not get ahead of ourselves just yet, ladies," Red said, holding her hand up to get the girls' attention. "NaTasha and Monique, I'd like the two of you to take some notes."

Monique didn't move, so I asked Red for a piece of paper from her notebook.

"Are you girls going to need additional help?" Red asked.

"Actually, I asked Quiana to help us as well," Monique told her. She slapped five with Quiana and Rochelle. That was news to me. I prayed Quiana wouldn't just get in the way and make our task even harder.

"Okay, fine then," Red said, writing something down. "I expect you to fully cooperate and help one another out. I would hate for anything to go wrong during this planning time to remove either of you from our recognition list."

"You trippin', Red," Quiana said loudly. "I told my whole family I was getting out of here. You know I don't need to come here anymore. I got to get up out of here this time."

"Then I'm sure you'll work harder than anyone to help NaTasha, right?" Red said, smiling. I hoped Red would join us during every step of the planning process. I was asking for trouble being alone with those two.

"If it's our ceremony, why do we need NaTasha in the first place?" Rochelle asked. Some of the girls nodded in agreement. "She isn't even going to be recognized."

"Because she's willing to help," Red said quickly, but then added in her quiet voice, "and just as with everyone new you'll meet in your lives, you may learn something from one another."

The girls mumbled for second, but no one said anything else, except for Tilly. She had all but disappeared from the circle with her silence. She let go of my shoulder and leaned in toward the center of the group. All the sudden it was hard to breathe. Get them, Tilly!

The girls quieted and all eyes were on my grandmother. The scowls disappeared almost immediately, as if Tilly held some magic powers. She took a deep breath in and then slowly pushed all the air out.

"Red and I were in here together just like you girls now," Tilly started quietly. She was almost whispering. When I leaned closer to hear her, she had a look of sheer force in her eyes, determination. "We were at each other's throats day in and day out."

Red and Tilly looked at each other and smiled.

"We didn't know nothing about each other," Tilly continued. "I just knew I couldn't stand her. And she couldn't stand me, either."

The girls and I stared at Tilly and Red. It was hard to imagine the two fighting like Quiana and Monique and I were now. They were so close these days. I wondered what huge event had made them become friends. I could tell the others were thinking the same thing.

"We didn't even speak, just started fighting," Red said, taking over. "It almost got us kicked out of here, too. We were on our way to juvenile hall before we realized what we were doing. It was a bunch of silliness."

Tilly had run away from home a few times and her parents finally called the police on her. Red's story involved more serious crimes, but they both ended up at Amber's Place together. They each shared a little of their story.

Tilly's words stung. Hearing my grandmother spill her dirty laundry was embarrassing for me, especially in front of these girls. Tilly should have told me this stuff before, like back in Adams Park, or at least in the privacy of her apartment.

"It wasn't long before we had to sit down and work together," Tilly said. "The director at the time gave us a job to do and forced us to team up. There wasn't any person I wanted to get away from more, trust me. After awhile, we started talking and really got to know each other. The rest is history, I guess."

"That don't mean the same is going to happen with us," Quiana jumped in.

Tilly sat back, crossed one leg over the other, and folded her arms. I'd never seen her sit like that and she didn't really look comfortable at all. One leg looked like a dead tree limb, pushing the rest of the trunk over on its side.

"True, but who is to say it won't?" Tilly shot back. We looked around the circle at one another. Everyone looked back at me, except Monique. She was either asleep or really embarrassed.

"Maybe I should have told you girls earlier, but I didn't bring NaTasha here just by chance," Tilly said, completely shocking me. I didn't want to be talked about at all, and certainly not like I wasn't in the room. "She hasn't had the opportunity to find herself in the small, suburban town that she lives in, like you girls here in the city. The good Lord gave each of you a story, a different and unique story worth telling, and I believe He's giving you all a chance to figure it out together, just like me and Red here. It would be a real shame for you girls to keep on acting a fool and miss out."

A few more heads bowed and I wondered if Tilly would break out in prayer. She had done it before, so no one in the room would be surprised if she did.

"Tilly's right, ladies," Red said. "It is up to you to take the bull by the horns and make this work. Let's make this ceremony the very best it can be."

This was too much. Tilly was using me as an example. She and Red were talking about me like I wasn't even in the room. These girls had already done a good job of alienating me. Now my own flesh and blood was making it worse for me.

Red ran through a list of what we needed to prepare. I pulled a pen from my back pocket and wrote everything down.

"So, let's make a list of what you want to see at your reception," I said flatly. My voice was shaky.

"At my mom's graduation from City College, there were fancy tablecloths," Susan said. "She got to wear a robe, too. They had catered food from some big-time restaurant and they each got an invitation in the mail. They even had a prayer service and some of the graduates gave speeches."

"Sending out invitations?" Rochelle said, shoving Quiana next to her. "I ain't graduated from nothing in my life before that needed invitations."

A few of the girls giggled.

"Of course we can get invitations, Rochelle," Red said. "That's a great idea. Does anyone else have ideas?"

"You *know* I can do a prayer," Tilly said. Tilly could pray about anything at any time. The girls laughed. Out of the corner of my eye I could see Shaunda unfolding a piece of paper. "And, Monique," Tilly added, "we could have you do the speech, give someone else a chance to talk for a change."

Tilly looked right at Quiana, who twisted her face up after realizing the joke was on her. She smiled, though.

"No, I can't do all that," Monique said, with her head still bowed. "I get too nervous. Everyone will laugh at me."

"They're gonna laugh alright," Quiana said. "Maybe about how you look, but not about what's coming out of your mouth."

Everyone laughed at that. The girls sounded excited. Tilly looked at me and winked.

"I could help you write something," I offered to Monique. Quiana and Rochelle clammed up right away, but Monique looked interested. Quiana wrapped her arm around Monique, pulling her close like I was trying to steal her friend away.

"I can help, too," Quiana said with a challenging stare. I'd have to catch Monique later when her bodyguards weren't around.

"This is going to be great, ladies." Red said. "Who else has ideas?"

"What about an awards ceremony?" Shaunda asked, reading from her list. "Or a dance and a speech?"

So that's what her paper was all about. I nodded my head and wrote down her suggestions onto my own list. Now we were getting somewhere.

"Yeah, like an award for who used skin bleach the longest without anyone knowing?" Quiana whispered. Shaunda refolded her list and put it back in her pocketbook.

"Okay, Quiana, that's enough," Red said. "I'm glad most of you are on board to help NaTasha. It is my hope the rest of you will follow suit or the jokes will be all mine. I assure you."

Red dismissed us dramatically, pretending to call each name as if the girls were already onstage. The girls waved and bowed, then started gathering their belongings and moved the chairs back into place. The meeting had gone well, much better than I thought it would.

"Think about all we've talked about," Red said. "The more you plan, the better your ceremony will be. And, NaTasha,

Monique, and Quiana, you three may want to meet over the weekend sometime to exchange more ideas."

Red was pushing it.

"Yeah, we'll see, Red," Quiana said, before walking out of the room.

Sounded like my weekend plans of relaxing with Tilly had changed. Tilly grabbed my hand and we followed the others out of the room.

CHAPTER FOURTEEN

TILLY SENT ME outside early on Saturday morning. No grocery list, just told me to get some fresh air. It was early, but I wasn't the first one out. The neighborhood was bustling with people.

Store owners were lifting the iron security bars on their front doors and the street vendors were setting up for a long day of selling. I found Rex out on the corner.

"Good morning, Rex," I called out as I passed the bodega. He was leaning on a cardboard box, his cart not far away. He peeled a banana and waved it at me.

"It is a good morning, miss lady," he said, in between mouthfuls. I waited for him to keep talking. "How are the girls treating you up in the boogie down Bronx?"

"They're treating me just fine, Rex," I told him, thinking that overall they treated me horribly, but it was much better than the first few days I'd been there. I waved and kept moving. I was headed toward Central Park, where I was going to wander around until I was lost, and then try and find my way back home again. "Things may actually be looking up soon."

I paused and glanced toward the bodega.

"Well, that's good, Miss NaTasha," Rex said, leaning with me to see what I was looking at. He smiled. When he'd finished off the banana, he tossed it into a nearby trash bin. "He ain't working today."

"Who are you talking about?" I asked him, while he stood up and pushed his cart off in the direction of Tilly's building. "I was just trying to remember if we needed anything for dinner tonight."

He didn't stop pushing or turn around, just raised his arm up in the air and kept walking. He thought I'd really be looking into a store for that boy. Can't a girl check the aisles in a store for no reason at all?

I walked the few blocks toward the park, letting the wind blow my hair across my face. Tilly had helped me wash and blow-dry it last night. It resembled Bozo the Clown's, without the orange coloring. Tilly said it looked good, so I left it alone. My friends at home wouldn't be able to even recognize me. Since I'd arrived in Harlem I'd seen so many different hairstyles. No one looked the same. Here, my natural hair blended right in.

I rounded a trail that led to the top of a hill and looked out across an open field. By the time I got to the top, the sun had fully risen and spread its rays through the trees, creating shadows all around my feet. There was a small wooden bench, with slightly broken pieces. I sat down and got comfortable.

I took in all the sounds. They were sounds I used to hear back home, kids playing in the field below, leaves whispering in my ears, and birds singing songs from the trees above me. At Tilly's, most of the sounds were loud neighbors arguing in the street, police sirens blaring, screeching subway trains, honking taxis, and drivers with foul mouths. I thought about sitting in the park all day long. Tilly would probably enjoy her freedom without me under her feet for a few hours.

"Hey, stranger, I haven't seen you around in a few days."

I turned to the voice. It was Amir. He looked different in street clothes, without a white apron and butcher's hat on. His white T-shirt and baggy, khaki shorts were soaked with sweat and stuck to his body. He looked good.

I smiled and waved at him.

"How's it going?" he asked, wiping his brow.

"Still here," I said. I knew it was a silly thing to say as it came from my mouth, but it came out anyway. Of course I was there, with an old shirt on, no makeup anywhere on my face, and wild Bozo the Clown hair. I was glad he hadn't kept running past like he didn't recognize me. "I don't leave until the end of next week. You know I wouldn't leave without saying good-bye."

Amir smiled and walked closer to me.

"Good to know," he said. "Is it okay if I sit?"

Of course it was okay. He could have asked to lie across my lap and it would have been A-OK with me. I nodded my head and made space for him.

We sat in silence for a while, but I couldn't hear the birds, the leaves, or the kids laughing anymore. I couldn't hear anything, except Amir breathing heavily in and out right next to me. Our shoulders touched slightly. His skin felt nice, like a flower.

I hadn't been this close to a boy since Mr. Cook's science class. My partner, Hank Andrews, had a reputation for blowing up science experiments. He would sit close to me and say "watch this" and then light something on fire. Hank smelled like eggs. Amir smelled nothing like Hank.

When Amir looked away, I leaned closer to smell him.

"That bad, huh?" he said, catching me and laughing. He sniffed his armpit and made a face. "Yeah, it's bad. I don't always smell this good, I've been running for almost an hour already."

"No, no, it isn't that," I laughed. "Just making sure it wasn't Hank and eggs."

"Eggs?" he asked suspiciously.

"Never mind," I said, looking back out across the field. This was nice, me and Amir, in the park. I could stay up here all day long. "Do you run that long every day?"

"I try to," he said, relaxing again. "It's good exercise. It gives me an excuse to get out of the store and hang in the park. I do my best work up here."

I could feel Amir's eyes on me, like a zoomed-in telescope, only he was close enough to touch. I was happy to have his attention. I put up my hand to block his view and he laughed.

"You're beautiful," he said quietly. I wanted to pretend I didn't hear him the first time, so he'd say it again. "I don't mean to stare, but you are."

Beautiful. Only my mom and dad and Tilly had ever said that to me, and they didn't really count. Somehow it sounded different coming from Amir's mouth, more meaningful, sweeter even. I watched him for a minute. I liked the strong line of his jawbone and the small hairs around his top lip.

"Thank you," I said. He kept his eyes on me, dark, round, and powerful eyes, like he was examining every inch of my body. I was drawn in by their power and wanted to know more about him, his whole life story. A small scream from the trail nearby jolted us back to the park.

A little boy tripped in front of us and fell onto a rock. His left roller skate was stuck and he wiggled his ankle back and forth until it was free. The boy rubbed his sore knees and let Amir pull him up so he was standing again.

"Hey, you okay, little guy?" Amir asked. "Be careful going back down the hill."

The kid smiled and rolled back to meet his family, who had stopped to wait for him not far away. His parents waved and mouthed "thank you." Amir came back and sat down next to me, closer than he had been before, and nudged me with his shoulder. I dramatically pretended to fall off my side of the bench. He laughed and pulled me closer to him with both arms.

"My hero," I sang, teasing him.

"Oh, yeah?" he asked. "So, I guess now I get a reward, huh?"

The hairs on my arm stood straight up and rubbed against his and tickled me like feathers. All of a sudden I was very aware of the sun and heat beating down on us from above. I could feel sweat forming on my forehead and the back of my neck. I closed my eyes and took a deep breath, just as Amir leaned in and kissed me.

It must have been a dream, but when I opened my eyes he was there, pulling his lips gently off of mine. His lips were soft and felt nice. They tasted salty like nuts or lightly buttered popcorn. If I hadn't been out of breath before he did it, that kiss would have done the trick. I wanted him to do it again. My heart sped up a little, in anticipation of a follow-up.

"I hope that was okay," he said quietly. I was a little embarrassed. He'd kissed before, I could tell because he was so confident. Maybe I hadn't been what he expected, not having any practice and all. Of course it was okay. My first kiss and it was wonderful. "I've wanted to do that ever since I met you."

The spilled cans of beans flashed in my head and I opened my eyes wide. The embarrassment was enough to make me shy away, but I giggled instead. Amir watched me laughing and looked hurt.

"No, it's not you," I said quickly. "That was nice, great even. I was just thinking about the mess I made in your store the day I met you."

Amir started laughing, too. "I'd almost forgotten about that." Tilly was right. I shouldn't have reminded him. "It wasn't so bad. Actually, it was kind of cute."

There was nothing cute about acting a fool in front of a crowd, let alone a cute guy. He probably wouldn't be up on

this hill kissing me if he knew I'd made a habit of being fool-
ish back home, too.

"I was so embarrassed," I said, covering my eyes. "I
wanted to go straight back home after that but Tilly said I was
being silly."

"You *were* being silly," he said, nudging me again. "And if
you'd left, I wouldn't have gotten the chance to kiss you. Plus,
it has happened before, you know. I shouldn't have stacked
them so high, my fault."

"Yeah, right," I said, "I'm sure you're just saying that to
make me feel better."

Amir grabbed my hands and pulled me up on my feet. We
walked hand in hand down the hill toward a park exit.

"For what it's worth, I'm glad you stayed," he said when
we'd reached the street. The city engulfed us. The quiet of
the park disappeared immediately, like we'd stepped through
an invisible force field and into another world.

People were everywhere: some shopping, some with kids
running around them, and others just standing on the street
corners chatting. Busy taxi drivers sped by and the street vendors were loudly arguing prices. All of it should have bothered
me, but somehow for the first time it was comforting.

When we reached the corner of Tilly's block, Amir let go
of my hand and kissed me lightly, on the cheek this time.

"Would you like to see a movie with me sometime?"
he asked. I'd always thought my first date would be at an
amusement park or a romantic picnic, like on TV, but a
movie was good, too. I must have been making a strange

face without knowing it. "Or if you prefer, we can have dinner somewhere?"

"No, I mean, sure," I answered too quickly. Amir was confused. "A movie is fine, sounds like fun. I'd love to go."

"Great," he said, exhaling like he was relieved. "How's Monday for you? I'll stop by Tilly's around seven thirty to get you."

"Monday works for me," I said, smiling. So that was it, my first kiss, a walk in the park, and a date. It couldn't have been more perfect.

Even with everything that was between us, Heather was the one and only person I wanted to share this news with. I practiced how I'd tell her and pictured her response. I almost skipped the whole way home.

"So, what's up with you and ole boy?" Khalik was on his cell phone, but flipped it shut as soon as I'd reached the stairs where he sat with his legs spread wide in front of him, blocking the door to the building. "You didn't let him cast no spell on you, did you?"

I remembered Amir's touch and shivered a little, despite the heat. Khalik had an evil grin and started bouncing a basketball up and down against the steps.

"I don't know what you're talking about, Khalik," I said, sitting down near him on the stairs. I probably should have kept walking right to the door, but Khalik didn't look like he was ready to move.

Khalik bounced the ball over and over again and scrunched up his face like I'd offended him or something. "Yeah, I'll bet you don't." His phone rang and he checked the screen, but didn't answer it. He slipped the phone back into his pocket and went back to the ball.

"Don't want her to hear me in the background?" I asked, teasing him. Now we were even. He just smiled and looked right at me.

"I don't know what you're talking about," he said, mocking me.

"Yeah, I'll bet you don't," I said, in my lowest voice, trying to sound just like him. I swatted at his basketball and knocked it away from him. He laughed and we watched the ball roll down to the bottom of the stairs. He didn't move, so I jumped up to get it. I threw it up to him, right to his chest, and he looked winded.

"Damn, girl, you been lifting weights out here, too?" he asked, pretending to rub his sore chest. "You play some ball I don't know about?"

"Not really," I said, climbing the stairs again. At that moment I had a lot of energy, though, like maybe I could get out on the court with Khalik and play a game. "I play a little volleyball when I can."

He snorted. "Sounds like some white girl stuff to me," he said, laughing. Khalik threw his basketball high above his head and pretended to spike it. The ball fell in his lap, and he raised his arms in fake cheerleader style and pumped his fists.

"You've never seen black girls play volleyball?" I asked. Khalik shook his head no. His phone rang again. This time he switched the ringer to vibrate. "That's crazy, of course they do. Your girl Monique even plays. She was pretty good during our practice."

Khalik smiled at that, the kind of smile that had some history, or at least a good story behind it. I leaned closer to him and put my hand up to my ear, waiting for the story. He pushed my hand away.

"There's nothing to tell," he said, "and she ain't my girl."

"Okay, if you say so," I said.

"Yeah, I say so."

We sat and watched the street again. From where we were sitting, we could see the train station, a few clothing boutiques, a grocery store, a movie theater, and the courts. So much going on around us, but Khalik and I were on the sidelines, like we were benched for too many penalties in a game.

Rex wheeled his cart up from the bodega, with Tilly at his heels. Her bags were on top of the cart, full of food.

"How long you two lovebirds been sitting here?" Tilly asked us. My face got hot. Khalik smiled, but didn't say anything. We took Tilly's bags off Rex's cart. Rex wheeled over and sat down on the bottom step. Tilly held the door open while Khalik and I set the bags inside. "Woo, child, I must be getting old. And I didn't even make it to all my shops yet."

Tilly could shop all day, just like my mom. My mom bought purses and shoes to match the purses. Tilly spent hours searching through antique shops looking for glass animal figurines, or different-colored wigs and church hats. She'd spend hours looking, but would rarely buy anything.

"You don't look old, Ms. Tilly," Khalik said dutifully.

Tilly gave him her best "you bet I don't" look and slapped him on the arm. We all laughed.

"Thank you, baby," Tilly told him, batting her eyelids like a little girl. "I was just trying to convince Rex here the same thing, but what does he know?"

Rex had been sitting quietly, rearranging plastic bags on his cart. He turned around and looked Tilly up and down and said, "When you've lost it, you've lost it."

"Oh, shut up, you old fool," Tilly said, pretending to throw something at him. Rex and Tilly laughed together.

A car backfired on the street and we all jumped. It sounded like a bomb. Black smoke rose in a steady stream from the back of the car, but it kept speeding down the block. Tilly sucked her teeth. "That's a shame, all that noise."

"At least it wasn't a gunshot," Khalik said quietly. I wondered if his heart had just skipped three whole beats like mine had.

"You're right, Khalik," she said. "But never mind that. Tash, you been gone so long, girl, I thought you'd caught a bus back to the suburbs."

Tilly cracked herself up then. She obviously didn't remember being the one who sent me out so early. Her head and shoulders shook while she laughed. She almost looked like a bobble head. I loved watching her laugh. It always made me laugh, too.

"From what I hear, she had a really good time," Khalik said. He rubbed his chin and turned toward me. Tilly turned to me, too. Rex even leaned in. I rolled my eyes at Khalik but he just smiled and seemed to enjoy watching me squirm. "Come on, Tash, tell us all about it."

I wanted his basketball right at that moment so I could send it sailing right into his chest again, but it was too far out of my reach.

"I went up to the park and took a nice, long walk and then came home," I said. Khalik gave me a look. Either he was gonna spill it or I should. "Oh, and I saw Amir while I was there, so we hung out for a little bit."

Khalik grinned like he'd just won some championship.

Tilly's eyebrows went sky-high and she grinned, the kind of grin she makes when she knows there's more to the story. Rex finished folding and refolding his bags and packed up to leave.

"Catch you all later," he called and waved good-bye. I should have run and jumped on the cart to escape.

"Alright, Rex," Khalik said. Tilly and I waved.

On any other day Khalik would have been running up and down the court with his boys. Now that I had news for Tilly's ears only, his friends were nowhere to be found.

"Boy, why are you here hanging on this stoop?" Tilly asked Khalik, reading my mind. "Your friends go off and leave you or something? Or did you find someone you were more interested in today?"

She looked at me when she said it. Khalik rolled his eyes.

"No, Ms. Tilly," he said, "it ain't even like that. I just felt like laying low for a minute. I'll probably get up with them later on. Here they go calling right now. I'll catch you later, Ms. Tilly. NaTasha."

He flipped open his cell and went into the building. Thank God. Enough humiliation for one day.

"Alright, girl, now come on with the gossip," Tilly said.

CHAPTER FIFTEEN

TILLY WAS STILL asking me questions about Amir while we got ready for church the next morning. She wanted to know all the details. And she had a whole first date meal planned by the time I was done telling her.

"You're so embarrassing, Tilly," I said. Once she made up her mind about something, her plan was final. We walked out the door with only a few minutes to spare.

"Girl, we'll be lucky if we get a seat," she said, walking to church as fast as she could go. She had on a blue and yellow flowered dress and held the matching blue feathered hat under one arm.

"Tilly, do that many people even go to church anymore?" I asked, trying to catch my breath from running after her. Back home, my parents and I hadn't been in years. "There can't possibly be a full house already."

Tilly just grunted and kept walking. We turned the corner a few blocks from her apartment and ran into a line of people, women in church hats, men in three-piece suits, and little kids in their Sunday best. Ushers in black suits and white gloves were keeping order on the street. A tour bus even pulled up out front and began letting the passengers off for service. Tilly passed by the end of the line and walked up the stairs into Hope Baptist Church.

"Tilly, why are so many people waiting to get inside?" I asked her, as we took seats in the first row of the church. "And how in the world did we get seats in row one?"

"Girl, the Lord is going to show up, so people want to be here to receive Him," she said. "And they always sit the elders up front. Thank the Lord because my sight is going anyway."

Tilly's sight was 20/20. I made a face to let her know she was full of it. She pretended not to see me and raised her hands like she was praying. I left her alone and watched more believers flow into the church. A young mother set her baby's car seat into place on the pew next to her. A heavyset older man and his much thinner and younger wife, both dressed in black suits, took bulletins from the usher and began to fan themselves. It was warm in the sanctuary.

A dark-skinned woman dressed in all white, from her large hat with a feather down to her pantyhose, stood at attention near the front pulpit and looked like she was waiting for someone. People filed in from the back doors and filled the pews quickly. All the people waiting outside weren't going to have seats. The place was packed.

The pastor walked in and raised both his arms and the crowd stood.

"Good morning, church," he bellowed from the pulpit. A

team of large men in black gym suits, who looked like body-guards, surrounded the pastor as he led us all in prayer. I bowed my head. "Let the church say, 'amen.'"

"Amen."

"Church, God is good," the pastor asked. He dropped his arms and motioned for us to sit.

"All the time," the congregation answered in unison.

"He's so good all the time and I'm here to tell you about it," he preached. "Do you want to hear about it?"

"Yes, tell it, pastor," the people responded.

"God is so good. He woke me up this morning to see this beautiful sun and to feel this summer heat. He gave us power, joy, and sound minds this morning, church."

"Yes, amen," Tilly said, almost rising to her feet. She waved a paper fan adorned with a funeral home advertisement on the back, and blew air toward me. I unbuttoned two buttons on my shirt and wiped some sweat from around my collar.

"He has blessed us with a wonderful church family and has brought each of us a mighty long way," he said.

The bodyguards looked around nervously as the pastor paced across the stage.

"Yes, He has," the young mother behind us said. Her baby woke up and began to cry softly. She set him in her lap and continued to listen. I couldn't help noticing she had on a pair of jeans and a large sweatshirt.

Tilly always said the Lord didn't care what we had on for church, but we should dress our best just in case this was the day He came to take us to our new home in Heaven. She said she didn't want to be caught dead in an old dress when she met her maker.

The music began to play and the people stood to their feet. I swayed and clapped along while choir members in long maroon-and-white robes began to file around the pulpit. They rocked the building from their dancing and their boisterous voices. It was beautiful. I looked at Tilly. She had her eyes closed and her hands lifted in the air.

The choir sang three more songs.

"Amen, church, you can be seated," the pastor said when they ended.

We all sat and opened our Bibles. The pastor read from the books of Ecclesiastes and Luke.

"Church, we are beginning a new season in the Lord and we need to live as leaders and examples for those who do not yet know Him," he told us.

I followed along and nodded when Tilly nodded. The pastor was right. This was a new time in my life. Some changes would have to be made in order for me to be okay: new friendships, new relationships, and a new attitude.

"Amen," I said along with everyone else.

After the service, Tilly moved down the main aisle like a celebrity. She waved to folks in the balcony and shook hands with people like she was the one who had given the sermon. More people came to talk with her than the pastor, who waited patiently on the pulpit for anyone wanting prayer.

"Hey, Ms. Rose," Tilly said, hugging a small woman wearing a large church hat. The lady only stood as tall as Tilly's shoulder but her voice made up for it. I swear they heard her voice all the way in the next church. I wondered if she had a hearing aid in her ear. She held on to Tilly as they talked. "Are you cookin' tonight, Ms. Tilly?"

"You know I'm cooking, girl," Tilly said, smiling proudly. Everyone knew about Tilly's food. "I'll be ready for you about five. My granddaughter here is going to help me get ready."

I smiled and shot Tilly a look. How could she be standing here telling tales in church? She knew all I could do was boil water.

"It's nice to meet you, dear," Ms. Rose yelled at me. "You remind me of my own granddaughter. Maybe I'll bring her with me tonight."

"Alright, Ms. Rose." Tilly pulled me out of the sanctuary. We made our way through the rest of the crowd and stepped out onto the street.

We walked slowly back to her apartment, with Tilly holding on to me and humming the whole way. We passed her place and headed into the bodega. Her smile widened with every step. I prayed for empty aisles and bad tunes, so maybe Tilly wouldn't dance through the store and embarrass me this time.

"Hey, Amir," Tilly sang, "hook me up with some meat, baby."

"You got it, Ms. Tilly," he said, slicing a turkey for her. He winked at me while he weighed the meat on his scale. My cheeks were hotter here than out in the sun. I stood in one spot so I wouldn't bang into anything and watched Amir's strong arm muscles flex while he cut into more meat. "Did NaTasha tell you about Monday?"

She pretended not to know and smiled like she was about to find out some juicy gossip about me.

"Not everything, my dear, so why don't you fill me in," she said, leaning onto the glass in between us. Amir looked at me to make sure it was okay. He looked nervous. It was cute. *Very* cute.

"Well, I was going to take NaTasha to see a movie," he stammered. "I mean, if that's okay with you, Ms. Tilly."

He just scored major points with her and probably didn't even know it. She beamed like he'd just proposed marriage. She glanced over at me and nodded her head.

"Of course it's okay," she said, taking the meat he handed her. "I was wondering what was taking you so long to ask her."

"Oh, Ms. Tilly," he said. "See you both on Wednesday."

I made an exaggeratedly slow three-point turn toward the door and could hear Amir laughing behind me. I pumped my hips with every step just for effect. I wasn't going to be remembered for the spilled beans forever if I could help it.

We got back to the apartment and Tilly put on an apron right away. I wrapped one of her aprons on, too, just to make her laugh. She saw how big it was on me and shook her head.

"You finally ready to learn how to cook, huh?" she asked, swinging a dish towel at me. I laughed and shook my head no. I started collecting dishes to set the table. Sundays after church were always a busy time around Tilly's apartment. "Girl, take that off, you look silly."

Tilly started humming one of the hymns we had just heard during service. I watched her measure sugar levels with her finger, choose the right turkey legs to cook, and adjust the stove temperatures. She was really at home in the kitchen, and I admired her for that. She'd found something she loved.

With the exception of cooking, I was just like her, from our round hips, to our attitude, to our coarse hair. For the first time I could remember, I was okay with all of it. I wanted to be just like Tilly.

"I love you, Tilly," I said. She turned and looked at me.

"You know I love you, too, baby," she said, flinging some sticky flour at me. I pulled some of it out of my hair. She nodded at my head. "You want me to fix your hair for you later?"

The last time Tilly braided my hair, I came away with small bumps around the edges of my scalp and tears in my eyes. She had sworn she wouldn't pull or twist too tight, but she lied. Those braids stayed in for a good two weeks and so did the pounding headache. They looked beautiful on my oval-shaped head, but I was like show and tell at school. The kids pointed and touched and stared like they'd never seen anything like it before. I had a feeling I wouldn't have that same problem here. All of a sudden, I missed having my hair done, pressed or braided.

"Sure, Tilly, if you don't mind," I said, placing all the forks on the right side of the plates. I lit the apple-scented candle in the center of her table and pulled the matching knives and spoons from the silverware drawer.

"Course I don't mind, honey," she said, smiling. She added another layer of butter flavoring to the turkey legs and slid the tray onto the center rack in the oven.

Soon the cooked turkey legs were cooling on the stovetop, green beans were boiling, black beans and rice were on a slow boil in their pots, too, and I was kneeling in between Tilly's legs getting my hair braided. Tilly hummed a fast hymn and parted my hair with enthusiasm. She had a comb in one hand, holding the hair in separate sections, and grease in the other hand, moisturizing my scalp.

"You know what design you want?" she asked just as the doorbell rang. I didn't know. I thought about the elaborate hairstyles I'd seen at Amber's Place and around Tilly's neighborhood over the past few weeks. I knew what I didn't want, but I was okay with Tilly choosing a style for me. The twists she wore looked elegant. I told her something simple and cute, and got up to answer the door.

"Ooh wee, girl, look at that head," Ms. Rose yelled to me. "Your stuff was flying in church, but, girl, ooh wee. You want me to fix you up real quick before we eat?"

Did everyone in Harlem know how to do hair except for me? I invited Ms. Rose inside and she hugged me tightly, so tight I almost missed seeing Shaunda slip past me. Ms. Rose let me go fast.

"You two girls know each other, right?" Ms. Rose asked, grabbing Tilly up next.

Of course we knew each other and I was slightly relieved it was her, and not one of the other girls. I just hadn't expected Shaunda, who hugged Tilly and grabbed a seat on the couch across from all the hair products.

"Um, yeah, we met at Amber's Place," I answered her, smiling at Shaunda.

She returned my smile but didn't say anything. I took a seat back in front of Tilly and she started to braid.

I tried to keep my eyes on Ms. Rose and Shaunda, but Tilly had my head gripped hard like a football tucked in her arms. It was painful but I knew Tilly wasn't trying to hurt me. I closed my eyes and listened to Ms. Rose and Tilly talk about the church building fund and the women's missionary board, both of which Ms. Rose was in charge. Most of the conversation was gossip about nosy women volunteers, missing money, and slack members.

Shaunda and I were quiet the whole time.

"I told you not to get so involved, Rose," Tilly told her, laughing about the ten-year-long building fund project with no construction work in sight. "You and I both know they ain't building nothing in there but a new tour route for the visitors."

They both laughed. I heard Shaunda giggle, too, and shuffle through one of Tilly's magazines. I wondered what she was really thinking about. Had she been in Tilly's house before? Was she collecting stories about Tilly and me to share with the other girls? Had any of the other girls been in Tilly's apartment before? All the questions started a panic deep in my chest and a headache worse than the pain from the tight plaits Tilly was folding on my head. I was so deep in thought I didn't even hear Ms. Rose talking to me. Tilly flicked the comb against my forehead and they all laughed at me.

"Huh? What? I mean yes?" I stammered, holding my hand against my forehead. They continued laughing. I caught Shaunda looking around at the paintings on the walls and the books I'd stacked into Tilly's bookcases over the years. She wouldn't have done that if she'd been there before. I took a deep breath until my heartbeat slowed to a normal pace again.

"I was just asking how things have been going for you at Amber's Place," Ms. Rose repeated herself. The sides of her lips quivered when she spoke. "Shaunda here has told me all about you, I feel like I know you already."

I looked over at Shaunda to search her eyes, to no avail.

My heartbeat sped up again. I wanted to know exactly what she told her grandmother. My volleyball skills probably got left out, but the fighting and the teasing? I pulled away from Tilly for a second to take a break. I hadn't even told Tilly the full story yet, and now her friends already knew.

"Don't worry, only the good stuff," Ms. Rose said with the quivering lips. "I couldn't bribe the juicy stuff out of her. She's a good girl this one, now anyway."

Ms. Rose patted her granddaughter's knee like you would a puppy dog. Shaunda ignored her and kept flipping through the *Jet* magazine she had been reading. I couldn't picture her as the self-destructive, troubled teen that Shaunda referred to. But she was in there somewhere.

"It's been rough, but I think I'm finally starting to fit in," I said. Ms. Rose and Shaunda didn't look convinced. Tilly even tightened up on my hair.

"Is that what you've been trying to do up there, fit in?" Tilly stopped halfway through a braid and pulled my head around to face her. She knew I was trying to fit in, anywhere and everywhere. "Is that what these braids are about? Because that ain't the reason I brought you here, to be somebody else. You're supposed to be up there learning about yourself."

"No, Tilly, that's not what I'm trying to do," I told her. She kept mouthing something under her breath. I could see Shaunda looking over to hear what Tilly was saying. "Let's talk about it later, alright, please?"

Tilly finished braiding but kept talking about what a shame it would be for me to have wasted my time here. I didn't want to be any of those other girls; it was just easier to not stand out so much all the time. She just didn't understand.

Ms. Rose and Tilly kept talking about how fitting in was the wrong way for me to go. Shaunda even chimed in a few times. What did she know? She was acting odd, but I couldn't put my finger on it. I didn't really want to pay too much attention. I was just glad Tilly didn't leave my head halfway unbraided. The girls at Amber's Place would get a kick out of that.

We sat to eat and the grandmothers still wanted to discuss my fate.

"She'll learn one day," Ms. Rose said, as if I wasn't even in the room. Tilly had a tendency to do that, too. "Maybe not this time, but it will happen."

"I know that's right," Tilly said, stuffing a loose piece of turkey in her mouth. "That's what I prayed for."

Praying about my social standing was going too far. God surely didn't have the time.

"Tilly, please," I begged, "can't we talk about something else?"

"How about our volleyball match? NaTasha is pretty good," Shaunda offered. This girl was never coming to dinner again. She might as well have given a play-by-play demonstration of how the girls almost killed me with a volleyball.

"Or, how about the beautiful weather we're having?" I asked, looking at Shaunda again.

"Funny you should bring that up," Tilly said, smirking. "I heard it was supposed to storm tonight."

"That's too bad. It was such a beautiful day," Ms. Rose said.

It was too easy to distract two women who liked to talk a lot. It didn't really matter the subject. They just liked to talk. A few times I found myself zoning out of their conversation. Thinking about Amir was more fun.

Shaunda wasn't paying much attention to them, either. She might as well have not been there at all. Her grandmother probably forced her to come anyway. This girl sitting at Tilly's table was almost a different person from the one I knew at Amber's Place. I wanted to know what was going on, but without our grandmothers around to intervene.

"Shaunda, you want to sit out on the stoop for a while?" I asked, interrupting all flow of conversation going on next to us. Shaunda looked up and only grunted an answer that I couldn't hear. But we cleared our plates and started down the stairs.

"So, what's up with you tonight?" I asked. "Why are you here?"

"What are you talking about? My grandmother said you wanted me to be here," she said, looking at me like I had a third eye on my forehead.

"She did, did she?" I asked. I was going to kill Tilly. No way did I want Shaunda in my personal space, especially acting like she didn't even know me. Just a few days ago, she was willing to tell me all I needed to know to survive. "Why are you acting so funny anyway?"

"I don't know what you're talking about, NaTasha," she said, rolling her eyes and looking down the block. The sweet, helpful girl who'd shared a locker and all her dark secrets with me had clearly left the building.

"Did I do something to offend you, Shaunda?" I asked, sounding desperate and insecure. I didn't care.

"No, you didn't *do* anything," she said. But her tone said the opposite.

"So, if I didn't do anything, what then?" I asked, getting frustrated and a little nervous. "I thought we were friends."

"I don't have any friends, NaTasha," she snapped. The muscles in her neck were strained and she looked close to tears. "I thought we were friends until you turned into one of them."

"One of who?" I asked.

This girl might be the craziest one of them all. She couldn't mean Quiana, Rochelle, or Monique, or she was dumb, too.

Since when was I a part of any group at Amber's Place? This had to be some kind of misunderstanding. She must have seen the confusion on my face.

"I was the one who talked to you, not them," she said. She was really mad. "Now they talk to you and about you and still, no one notices me. No one sees me anywhere. You step in and overnight, you're the star of the show. I guess I got what I asked for, huh? And I bet Red didn't even consider putting me in charge."

It was just a guess, but Red might have already seen this unstable side of Shaunda. It was clear that she was serious, but I couldn't wrap my brain around her being so upset by my helping out with the reception.

Shaunda, who looked like a supermodel, was jealous of me. It made no sense.

"Yeah, but they're torturing me," I said, defending myself. If she only knew I would rather trade her places. It would be easier to be invisible. "You've seen them, they treat me like crap."

"Yeah, but they *see* you," she said, softening her voice. She let the tears roll down under her nose and chin. I didn't know what to say.

"Shaunda, you're so beautiful, you can't possibly think that no one notices you," I said. I wasn't sure if my words would make her feel any better, but I wasn't sure what else to say. She held up her hand to stop me. She wiped her face and neck with the palms of her hands, drying them on the thighs of her dark blue skinny stretch jeans.

"It's okay, I've learned to live in the shadow," she said. "I've been there my whole life."

She had no idea how much we really had in common.

Before I said anything else, Tilly and Ms. Rose came bounding through the front door. We stood and I exchanged hugs with Ms. Rose, while Shaunda stood to the side with her head down. Tilly and I watched them both walk down the street.

"That was nice, huh, baby?" Tilly asked, nudging me. "Everything okay out here between you two?"

"Yeah," I said, and that's all I could say.

"Looks like you're finally making some new friends," she said.

Tilly seemed so happy that I nodded.

By the time we got back upstairs, the sun had completely set and the dishes were already cleared and washed. I picked up the phone to call my parents.

"Tash, baby, we miss you so much," my parents said, almost in unison. It was good to hear their voices. It was good to think about my home again.

"What's going on at home?" I asked excitedly. I wanted to hear how much everyone missed me. Dad said work was good. Mom said the shopping was a bore and asked about the pocketbook I was supposed to find for her. I had actually forgotten all about it. I told her I'd start shopping for it soon.

"So, has Tilly given you enough black history lessons yet?" my dad asked, and we all laughed. I filled them in on everything.

I should have left out a few details, like the fighting and name calling, but I didn't. I even told them about dinner with Shaunda and my park time with Amir.

"So, I guess you are having a good time after all," my mom said sadly.

"You sure you're alright up there?" my dad asked. He needed to hear me say it. "It sounds a little too dangerous to me, to be getting so involved. Remember, you're coming home soon, but you can come home sooner if you want to."

"Yeah, your friends are ready for you to be home. They even stopped by to drop something off for you," my mom added. What friends? Heather was the only one who ever visited. "Heather came by, and Stephanie was with her the last time."

The conversation quickly took a turn for the worse.

No way could I go home now even if I wanted to. My worst enemy would be waiting at my door when I returned. I hoped Heather didn't think Stephanie and I would all hold hands and skip down the block together. That girl had treated me like fresh dog poop and now she was stopping by my house and talking to my family?

"You know, I'm really okay up here," I told them, rushing them to get off the line. "It's really not that bad. And I'll be home in no time."

"Just come home in one piece, okay, kiddo?" My dad got the hint. We were almost done. My mom had a harder time saying good-bye.

"It sounds like Tilly's put you to work up there, huh?" she

asked. I ignored her. How could she have welcomed Stephanie into our home? I wanted no part of it.

"I love you guys," I told them. We blew kisses through the phone and they asked to speak to Tilly. I handed the phone to Tilly and ran to punch a hole in something.

I THOUGHT ABOUT Shaunda and her sob story. Not only did I need to plan a reception for these girls, but now I felt guilty for doing it and personally responsible for Shaunda, too.

But how could I possibly help her when I couldn't even solve my own problems? My best friend had turned against me. My enemy befriended my best friend. I had no reason to go back home.

I stepped out of Tilly's apartment with renewed strength. I might as well plan a wonderful party while I was here.

"What's got your thoughts all in a bundle, my dear?" Tilly asked me on the way out of her apartment. No one could understand the thoughts going through my head. Not my mother. Not Heather. Not Quiana, Amir, or even Tilly. We walked down the sidewalk quickly and made it to the station just as a train was pulling to a stop.

"Nothing I want to even try and explain right now," I told her. She looked hurt. "Hey, Tilly, you know what? Go on without me. I have a quick stop to make."

She knew I was keeping a secret from her. But not one she needed to know about right away. I hugged her and promised to meet her uptown in less than an hour.

"One hour. I mean it, girl," she said sternly. "And then I'm sending someone after you. Mark my words."

"Don't worry, I'll show up, I just have something I need to take care of," I told her. I knew she was serious. The wrinkles between her brows were scrunched. But I had no intention of being late. The conversation I intended to have would only take a few minutes.

I walked to a corner store in the opposite direction. I bought breakfast and started combing the streets. It only took me twenty minutes to find him. Rex was squatting behind the basketball courts.

"Well, well, well, look what the cat drug in this fine morning," he said, smiling. He looked like he hadn't slept all night. Every piece of clothing he wore was tattered down to the last thread, like he'd been through a paper shredding machine. I set a package of blueberry Pop-Tarts on top of the shopping cart where all of his life possessions were piled.

"I'm still here," I said. "Hey, Rex, how are you?"

"Good for you," he said, sort of ignoring my question. "We need the nice folk like you to stay around this neighborhood. Seems like everyone grows up and moves away. Not me, I'm staying around forever."

Rex always said something to make me feel better. It never dawned on me that someone like Rex could have so many important things to say. There was always a deeper meaning behind his words.

"I'm good now," he said, ripping the Pop-Tarts open. "Were you looking for me?"

"Yeah, actually I was," I told him. He took a giant-sized bite from the first Pop-Tart. A few crumbs fell from his lips. "I had something I wanted to ask you."

"Okay, shoot," Rex said. He turned so he was facing me. "What is it?"

He smiled and finished the rest of his breakfast while I pitched my idea to him. He was very patient and let me finish all I had to say. Every few minutes he nodded his head or grunted a little in response, but that was it. When I was done, he smiled a little, stood, and rolled his cart off down the street.

About ten feet away he said, "Very interesting indeed," but never turned around.

I arrived in the Bronx with fifteen minutes to spare, but I rushed to find Tilly so she would stop worrying. I found her in the multipurpose room with the rest of my nonenthusiastic planning committee. Shaunda, Susan, and Maria were lounging on a sofa with books close to their noses. Rochelle and Monique were browsing through a *Black Hair* magazine. Quiana was nearby in a corner alone, twirling a cigarette around and around in her fingers. Tilly, Coach, and Red were in another corner talking.

I looked around the room. We weren't that different at all. I just had to convince the girls we could work together.

"Ooh wee, look, everybody." Rochelle lowered the magazine. "Someone finally got a makeover. Self-discovery is a beautiful thing."

Rochelle and Monique cracked up laughing. I ran my fingers through the braids Tilly had put in my hair and walked around them to have a seat with the other girls. Rochelle stuck out her foot like she was going to trip me, but I saw her first and stepped over. She wiped tears away from the corners of her eyes, she was laughing so hard.

"Your hair looks really pretty like that, *mami*," Maria said, smiling at me. She made space for me on the couch and I sat down. Susan smiled, too, agreeing with her.

"Yeah, it sure does look pretty," Rochelle said, "looks like someone wanted to look just like you, Quiana."

The girls started laughing again. They did look a little like her braids but it was a completely different design. Quiana wasn't the type of girl to be flattered by copycats.

"Actually, it looks decent," Monique said, not looking up from the magazine. I knew she wasn't reading anymore, because Rochelle had half of it folded in her hands. Rochelle and Quiana looked at her, but no one said anything.

Red walked over to us then to make sure we had an idea of what we needed to get accomplished for the day. "You don't have long, ladies, so I would get down to business if I were you."

Red reminded us that everyone had a role to play in the planning and we should be open-minded and willing to listen. After that, she was gone, and she took Tilly and Coach with her.

The floor was mine and all eyes were on me, some squinted, some slanted, some wide-eyed, but they were all on me. I could feel my heart beating through my shirt.

"Well, who knew? Sellout hasn't given up yet after all," Quiana said loudly. "Still think you can pull this off?"

"Yep, and you're gonna help me," I said, with my shoulders back, ready for an attack.

"We'll see," she said, spitting sarcasm like venom.

"You have something I want and I have something you want, so we might as well work together," I told her, ignoring all the *oohs* and *aahs* coming from the other girls. Those were fighting words, but I hadn't meant them to come out so harshly. I braced for a hit. She sized me up for a minute and laughed it off.

"Let's get to work before you make me mad, Sellout," she said. And that was it. It was time to work. I was jumping up and down inside at my small victory with Quiana.

"Okay, I made a list of some things for the reception," I said, my voice shaking a little. "Let me know if any of these things appeals to you."

I read from the list about floral decorating ideas, menu varieties, and guest speakers. With every word out of my mouth, I heard a new sound.

"We could have . . ."

Sneeze.

". . . um, salmon and rice."

Cough.

"Or we could have . . . chicken and salad."

Hiccup.

"Roses are nice and appropriate for the . . ."

Another sneeze.

Finally, I just stopped reading.

"Well, that was a lovely list," Rochelle said, "but I'm sure we have better ideas."

She slapped five with Quiana and reached to do the same with Monique. Monique ignored her.

"I like the idea of roses," she said, shocking everyone. I wrote down *roses* and watched a few heads nodding in agreement. "We could use them on the tables around the food and around the stage area."

I wrote that down, too.

"And how about matching outfits for all the girls?" Maria added, holding on to her stomach. She shifted in her seat. "Or how about robes? We could wear blue robes with pink ribbons."

This was great. I wrote every idea down and listened to the girls argue about the blue and pink ribbons. No one liked that idea except for Maria, but everyone was involved. Even Quiana jumped in a few times to add her two cents.

"There ain't no way I'm wearing a robe," she said, leaning all the way back in her seat and stretching her legs out in front of her. "That would look crazy anyway, Maria. Why don't you just sit back and take care of that baby?"

Maria made a face, and shifted again in her chair. She rubbed her hands across her forehead and her belly.

"I would like to hear our names read at a podium," Susan

said quietly, almost so softly that we had to lean in to hear her. "When my brother graduated from college they had a podium, a large screen, and some guy was saying their names. It was exciting, like the start of a basketball game or something when they call out the team names."

Her face was red and she was really excited about it.

I looked around at each girl and everyone had smiles. Finally, one thing we all agreed on. I wrote that down, too.

"That is the dumbest idea I've ever heard," Quiana said, folding her arms.

"Well, I haven't heard you come up with anything better," I said, a little too quickly. All the laughter stopped. Quiana uncrossed her arms. I wasn't scared anymore. "Well? Let's hear your ideas if you have them, Quiana."

I had a full list of great ideas. Quiana had laughed at all of them. She had to come up with something better or I didn't want to hear from her. If she didn't want to get recognized for helping me, that was fine, but I had decided this reception was going to be a nice one, with or without her.

The girls waited for what seemed like an eternity and they all looked as shocked as I felt. We waited and waited and waited to see what Quiana was going to say — more important, what Quiana was going to do.

She had her fists twisted up into balls, but loosened them again.

"If you're going to recognize me, I want some of my home girls doing it," she said roughly. And that was it. Little did she know she came up with the best idea I had written down. I looked at all the girls sitting around the circle and knew exactly who to assign that responsibility to.

I wrote it in my notebook along with the other ideas and smiled at her. She scowled at me and sat back again. We went back to talking about flowers.

Maria wanted sunflowers and shifted in her seat again. When Monique suggested lilies, Maria cried out louder than all of us. She grabbed her stomach and fell out of the chair.

"Maria!" Quiana was on her feet fast. She and Rochelle pulled Maria back up onto the chair and I ran for help.

CHAPTER SEVENTEEN

AMBER'S PLACE WAS eerily quiet, almost like we were in a haunted house and were waiting for the ghost to jump from a dark closet and scare us. Tilly and Red had gone straight to Harlem Medical Center to check on Maria.

"She'll be alright, baby," Tilly had said after dropping me off, "she's having a baby, not dying. You girls carry on and plan a good show for her when she comes home."

We all knew Tilly was right, but the thought of Maria lying in a hospital bed alone was too scary. The girls piled into the main room of the center one by one, but no one made a sound, no loud music playing, no fighting, no talking trash, no talking at all.

Coach walked in shortly after all of us and blew her whistle even though she already had our full attention.

"Okay, ladies, for those of you who don't know, Maria is at the hospital," she started, forcing the words out of her mouth. The armpits of her T-shirt were soaked with sweat like she'd jogged five miles to meet us. "We don't have any news yet, but as soon as we know, you'll know, too. She's a month away from her due date, but I'm sure mom and baby will be fine. Business as usual until we hear otherwise."

I could feel the other girls eyeing me.

"Well, boss, what's it gonna be?" Susan asked, standing up and stretching. It was nerve-wracking having all the girls waiting for me to take charge. But we still had a recognition ceremony to plan for Thursday night. Strangely, though, I was okay with it. It would be a welcome distraction from thinking about Maria.

I motioned for the girls to follow me, but I pulled Shaunda to the side first and whispered in her ear. She grinned and followed the rest of us into a corner of the lounge area.

"Okay, let's talk about what we have so far so we can place orders today," I said. The girls jumped in like I was giving prizes for the most suggestions. After a few hours we'd gone through a mock program, chosen the food, assigned decorations to Rochelle and Monique and certificates of completion to Quiana and me. I was pleasantly surprised at how willing the girls were to help with the planning, everyone except for Monique. She sat quietly throughout the entire meeting with her head down.

"Monique, are you okay?" I asked, during a break.

"Yeah, it's nothing," she said, wiping a tear away.

"Are you sure?" I asked her, not knowing if I was the right person to be prying in her private business. When she didn't swing at me or call in her bodyguards, I sat down next to her.

She shook her head no, but started talking anyway. "He just won't leave me alone." I assumed she was talking about Gray Hairs, the loser boyfriend who showed up for visitor's day.

"What do you mean?" I asked.

"I told him I didn't want to go with him anymore and he flipped out," she cried. "He was waiting for me when I got home yesterday and said he's going to be waiting for me every day until I take him back. He's crazy."

I looked around to find one of her friends so they could help her. Of course, I was the only one around. Tilly and Red were at the hospital. Coach was in her office waiting for news from the hospital. The other girls had run to get snacks and have a smoke before we started again. It was only me.

"So, what are you going to do?" I asked.

"I don't know," she said. "I guess I just have to go back to him."

Monique wiped her face with a crumpled Kleenex. Clearly going back to her loser boyfriend wasn't the right choice, but I didn't know if she would want to hear it from me. No one else was around, so I had to say something.

"Monique, you don't have to go back to him," I said quietly.

She looked at me out of the corner of her eye.

"You don't know anything about my life," she said.

She was right. But I did know she shouldn't have to be in a relationship that was unhealthy or unsafe. There had to be another way.

"You're right, I don't know," I said, "but I'm worried about you."

"Don't be," she said sarcastically. "I'll be fine. I always am."

"Isn't there someone at home you can talk to?" I asked, feeling really sorry for her. If I had a problem like hers, I could go to Tilly right away. My parents would be there for me, too. "What about your family?"

She sucked her teeth and looked at me again. "My stepdad is the only one. He works a lot, and doesn't have time for my mess."

"What about talking to one of your friends here?"

She looked at me like I told her pigs were now flying.

"I thought they were your best friends in the world," I told her.

"Shows you how fake some people can be," she said. I could tell she was referring to herself. "All the girls here have some secret they are carrying around, including me."

"Most of my life I've been pretty fake, too," I said. I thought about dancing in Adams Park, competing to grow my hair like my white friends at home, and praying that I would wake up with lighter skin so the boys would like me.

I didn't know where the words came from, but my tears came from deep down inside. Monique was already crying, so we both sat quietly for a minute, just trying to understand each other's pain.

"I was so scared to come here," I told her. "But I'm learning it's easier just to be myself, because there's always gonna be someone like Quiana or Rochelle who won't like me. It just isn't worth it."

She didn't say anything, but I saw her nodding her head like she was hearing me.

"No hard feelings?" she asked, out of nowhere. It was her best attempt at an apology. She held her fist in front of me and I tapped hers with my own.

She handed me a Kleenex and I wiped my face dry. Truly I wanted to help Monique. Maybe Tilly or Red could talk to her.

"Can't you just decide for yourself not to see him anymore?" I asked. "I don't have any of the answers and I don't know what you're going through, but you seem like you've made up your mind about him already. That doesn't mean you have to go back."

"Yeah, I know," she said, "thanks for listening."

"Anytime," I said, dabbing my eyes. We had addressed so much in our moment but I wasn't sure we'd resolved anything. It was nice to hear her apology, but I wished I could give her more answers to her problem with her boyfriend.

The other girls joined us again and took their seats. Thankfully, they didn't notice anything.

"So, who's giving our speech on Thursday?" Quiana asked. Good question. We didn't have much time left and the details still weren't all in place. I turned right to Quiana and winked and she started waving her hands frantically like I was trying to spray her with cheap cologne. "Oh, no, you already know that I ain't doing it."

Everyone laughed. Monique kept her head low. Shaunda slowly raised her hand in the air, like she was waiting for a teacher to call on her, so I did.

"What?" I asked. "You want to do it?"

Shaunda nodded, but looked at the other girls cautiously.

"What could you possibly have to say in front of a crowd of people?" Quiana teased her. She leaned forward and pressed her elbows into her knees. "You can't even talk in front of us."

I thought she would have a meltdown, but Shaunda took a deep breath to calm herself.

"I have a voice and a story to tell," she said, more calmly than I would have been able to. I recalled our conversation on Tilly's stoop and prayed Shaunda wouldn't start crying. The girls would eat her alive. But she didn't cry, she narrowed her eyes and sat up straighter. "I thought I'd start off by telling everyone about how I was bullied for years, how I started believing the lies and began hurting myself, but that after spending time working on building my self-confidence here at Amber's Place, I no longer let other people's foolishness run my life. I'm the only one who can help me survive, no one else."

Her jaw was clenched and she looked directly at Quiana. The whole room shifted uncomfortably. She and Quiana were in some sort of staring match. I looked back and forth, waiting for one or the other to pounce, but neither did. Quiana nodded and slowly leaned back in her chair. Shaunda stayed put.

"Sounds like a good speech to me," Susan said, giggling and play-shoving Quiana, who laughed and jumped to her feet.

"Okay, I'm gonna catch you bitches later," Quiana said, moving toward the door.

"Wait, we're not done yet," I said quickly. I didn't think we'd get another planning session before the reception. We still had the certificates to do. I told her so.

"Well, I was supposed to check in on the boys an hour ago, so I guess you'll just have to go with me," she said.

Panic raced through my bones. Tilly would kill me for leaving the building without her knowing about it. Shaunda and Susan were going to stay to work on a speech. Rochelle was going home to work on decorations with her mom. So I packed up my things, motioned to Monique to come with us, and followed Quiana out the door.

On the way to Quiana's apartment, Monique told us the full story about her boyfriend, whom we'd all agreed to call L.B. (Loser Boyfriend). Quiana was so mad I thought she was gonna ditch us right away and go after him herself. She definitely didn't want Monique going home alone. I had a feeling Monique was too scared to go anyway.

Even though I had heard some of it before, I was so caught up in Monique's story, I realized I didn't recognize where we were anymore. I wasn't even sure what neighborhood. I was scared now. Tilly would not be happy about me wandering aimlessly with two of my not-so-friendly new friends, especially if I was lost. I thought about her story of being left in an unfamiliar part of the city.

I stared up at the row of tall brown high-rises in front of us that must have stretched for an entire mile. We stopped in front of one of them and Quiana pulled out keys and started walking toward the doorway. I stopped and looked around for a minute. No way was I going to be able to tell Tilly where I was.

There were bars on every window. There were even bars surrounding a single tree in a patch of grass near the doorway. The Dumpster in front of Quiana's building clearly wasn't in use, because there were dirty napkins and frozen ice wrappers all over the ground around it.

"What are you waiting on, a doorman?" Quiana and Monique laughed and held open a heavy steel door for me.

"Oh, no, I was just wondering where we were," I said, struggling to hold the heavy door. "I've never . . . um . . . been over here before."

Monique looked at Quiana and then back at me. I hoped I hadn't said anything to offend Quiana. The last thing I needed right now was for her to get upset and desert me.

"Yeah, I bet you haven't," Quiana answered, sucking her teeth. She waved her hand around like Vanna White. "Welcome to public housing. We're still uptown, north Bronx. Can you handle it, rich girl?"

I wanted to tell her I wasn't rich, but they wouldn't have believed me. I wrapped the strap of my purse over my head and across my shoulder and followed her into the dark entryway. My heart raced as a wall of hot air hit us from the elevator. I sucked a big gulp of smelly air into my lungs.

"Of course I can handle it," I said, stepping in before the doors crushed me. They weren't the doors that automatically opened with a sensor like the subway cars. These doors were waiting for victims. I took another, smaller breath, this time without using my nose.

"Hit floor eighteen for me," Quiana said. I hit the button and prayed all the way up. She watched me watching the buttons light up at every floor, and laughed.

"I should have brought my camera for this," she said, nudging Monique, both of them watching me. The air got heavier and the stench stronger as we got higher and higher off the ground. I was sweating like I had just left a sauna room. My T-shirt felt more like a soaked bathing suit.

I peeked through the small window on the elevator door around floor twelve but I couldn't see anything. When the doors opened on floor eighteen, I sprinted out like I was crossing a marathon finish line. Quiana rolled her eyes.

"I don't like small spaces," I said, wiping my forehead.

She opened the door to her apartment and motioned for us to go inside. Three teenage boys lounged on a sofa and hardly looked up from the movie they were watching. Monique and I excused ourselves and hurried past the television, but Quiana stood right in front of it, with her hands on her hips.

"Y'all know you ain't supposed to sit in front of that TV all day," she yelled like someone's mom would. "Did anyone get the mail or clean up the bathroom?"

The boys didn't move. One of them waved for her to move. While they were arguing I took a look around. The walls were painted black and there were more posters framed around the walls than I had seen in small video rental stores. It reminded me of an art gallery back home, except these pictures were of brightly colored naked bodies. No wonder the boys never left the apartment.

"You two want anything?" Quiana asked us.

We both shook our heads and followed her into her bedroom.

"Good," she said, "'cause we probably don't have nothing anyway."

I expected to see black wallpaper, voodoo dolls lined up on her dresser, and two Japanese swords crossed above her headboard. But Quiana's bedroom looked just like any other teenage girl's room, concert posters pasted onto a light tan wall, a purple-and-white striped comforter with pillows and shams to match. She also had framed artwork of a city landscape. She saw me looking around.

"What are you gawking at?" she asked.

"Oh, nothing, I like your room," I said, noticing the bars covering her windows.

"Yeah, whatever," she said. "Let's get these certificates done. I'm sure you're dying to roll up out of here."

Monique and Quiana got comfortable and found spots on her bed, like they had done it many times before. I dropped into a purple beanbag chair near the bed. I pulled out the same notebook I'd written all the other reception details in and waited for the ideas to start flowing.

"What are they going to say?" Monique asked after awhile. She pulled one of Quiana's pillows across her stomach and leaned forward onto it. Quiana chose a disc from a CD tower near her and pushed play. A jazz, hip-hop mix filled the room. This girl was full of surprises.

"That's what we're here to figure out, smart one," Quiana answered sarcastically. Somehow when she said something mean to Monique, I was the only one to notice. "How about 'Congratulations on serving your time,' or 'Great job on screwing up your life?'"

Red would really have a fit. I wanted something simple and to the point. Monique wanted something lengthy and difficult to sign on multiple copies. Quiana wanted to make jokes.

We put down the notebooks and just listened to the music for a few minutes. I put my head back and closed my eyes and pictured myself dancing around in circles.

One of the boys from the living room couch knocked on the door.

"What?" Quiana screamed over the music. The volume wasn't up that high. I think she just wanted to scream.

"We got anything to eat?" he yelled through the door.

"Did you go buy anything to eat?" Quiana asked in true Quiana fashion. I thought about Tilly in her apron in front of the stove. She would be cooking up some fancy meal if she wasn't still at the hospital. I wondered how Maria was doing. Tilly had promised to call with any news, but we hadn't heard from her yet.

"Nah," he yelled back.

"Then, nah, we ain't got nothing to eat," she said. She threw a pillow at the closed door and it landed on the floor next to me. I picked it up and threw it back. She gave me an evil look and then leaned back against her headboard the way she was before the interruption.

A slow song came on and Monique lost her mind. The tears started falling almost before the melody kicked in. Quiana and I both watched her. I didn't know what to say. I'm sure Quiana wanted to say something, but she didn't. On the second verse of the song, Monique grabbed some tissues and began to wipe the tears away.

"I'm done crying over him," she said, making sure every drop was gone. She gathered up her things and started heading for the door.

"Where do you think you're going?" Quiana asked her. I looked back and forth between the two, wondering what was going on.

"I was supposed to be home by now," Monique answered. "If he's there, I'll just have to deal with it. If not, I'm going to sleep and not answer my phone."

I didn't think that was a very good idea, but I didn't have any other solution for her. Tilly's place was crowded enough with her one bedroom full of antiques and my stuff scattered around her living area. I cleared my throat to get Quiana's attention so she would say something to stop her.

"NaTasha will go with you just in case," she said flatly.

My mouth fell open. Quiana had a wicked grin on her face, like she'd just gotten caught stealing a candy bar red-handed.

"No. It's okay, I'm cool by myself," Monique said, looking at me.

"I would go with you, it's just that . . ." I started. It was date night. I didn't want to tell her I had plans with someone else. That sounded selfish.

"It's just that what?" Quiana said, with the smirk still on her face.

Monique was paused at the door with her hand on the doorknob. They were both waiting for my answer.

"I have a date," I said, looking at Monique. "If you want, I can walk with you on my way."

She shook her head no, but she didn't open the door.

"You have a date with your head looking like that?" Quiana asked.

"It's fine," I said, trying to stay focused on planning.

"It's not fine. It looks a mess," she said, looking at the time clock next to her bed. "What time is the date?"

"I'm supposed to meet him at seven thirty," I told them. Two and a half hours to walk with Monique and then shower and get ready.

"Then I guess we have to work fast," she said, motioning for me to move closer to her. She pointed to something on top of her dresser of drawers. "Monique, hand me that brush and comb and sit down."

Monique did as she was told and so did I.

Quiana dug into my hair like it was a plate of spaghetti. She moved my head roughly and quickly, but not so it hurt me. I could feel the comb moving through each section of hair and her fingers pulling at each braid all over my scalp. While she braided they reminisced about earlier days at Amber's Place. I sat quietly and listened to their stories.

Hearing them made me think of Heather. I wondered if we would ever have anything to laugh about when I returned home. After an hour, Quiana turned me toward a mirror.

"It's done, Sellout," Quiana said. I turned and posed for a minute. Quiana had done an amazing job. There was a maze of braids on my head and they looked sharp. I was more excited about my hair than the date. "The certificates should say 'Congratulations, now is the right time to change your life.' Now, you two get out of my house. I'm sick of looking at you both."

I was still smiling from ear to ear. We got the work done. Monique was happy to be walking with me. Quiana had just done something nice for me. I wanted to ask when she would start calling me by my real name, but I quit while I was ahead. Baby steps.

CHAPTER EIGHTEEN

MY CELL RANG just as Monique and I made it to the subway station near Quiana's house. I tucked my subway card back inside my purse and fished around frantically on the bottom for my phone. I didn't want to miss a call from Tilly. It had been hours already since we'd heard from her. I caught her right before the voice mail kicked in.

"Tilly?" I yelled into the receiver. Monique frowned and pretended to plug her ears. I stepped away from her so I could hear Tilly better. "So, how's Maria feeling? How's the baby?"

"She's okay and the baby is fine," Tilly said. She sounded relieved and happy. I gave Monique thumbs-up and she nodded that she understood. Her face was still preoccupied and tense, though, and I could tell she was dreading going home. "The doctors are keeping her so she can rest. They're both doing fine."

"That's great, Tilly," I told her. "When are you gonna be home?"

Even though we would miss each other, I would have liked to see her before my date. She would know the right things to say and what not to say. Monique motioned to the watch on her arm and headed for the stairs.

"I'll be home in a bit, baby," Tilly said. "I want to make sure someone in Maria's family is gonna stay with her and then I'll be on my way."

"Okay, Tilly," I agreed, a little too sadly. I knew she could hear in my voice that I was disappointed. For the first time in my life, when I needed my grandmother, she wasn't there. I didn't like how that felt at all. "See you later."

"NaTasha?"

"Yeah, Tilly?" I asked reluctantly. I pulled my subway card out and joined Monique at the top of the stairs. A few passersby gave us dirty looks for blocking the entrance and pushed past us.

"I'm sorry I'm going to miss you before you leave for your date, baby," she said. I could tell she was sad, too. I felt bad for making that happen.

"It's really okay, Tilly. It's just a silly date," I said, trying to make us both feel better.

"It is not silly, and I wish I was there," she said.

"I know, Tilly, I know."

"Have a good time," she said, "and remember everything I've taught you."

I knew this was the part where she would tell me not to try to act like someone I wasn't and that it would be up to me to keep my morals and pride in place even when there were no adults around to watch me.

"I love you, Tilly," I told her, and flicked my phone closed.

Monique was already at the bottom of the stairs waiting for me in front of the single turnstile.

"Maria's fine," I told her. Monique smiled faintly and swiped her subway card. I followed her to the downtown platform and looked at her again. "Did you hear me? Maria's going to be okay."

The last part got lost in the noise when a train barreled past us at top speed, sounding like a category five tornado. We waited until it slowed down so we could hear each other again.

"That's really great. I'm happy to hear it," she said, stepping into an almost packed car. I followed her in and held on to the pole in front of me. Monique held the pole above her head. "I was just thinking how messed up it would be if I ended up in the hospital tonight, too."

I stayed quiet. She watched me carefully to see how I would respond.

"Just think, you would have done all this reception planning for nothing after all," she said, laughing. I started to second-guess my decision to let her go home alone. At this point, I was more worried than she seemed to be. She noticed she was the only one laughing and stopped.

"He's just not the type to give up so easily," she said. The train rattled and shook us violently. When it finally stopped I asked her if she wanted to come home with me. "No, I'll be fine. You've done enough. I'll see you in the morning."

"Yeah, see you in the morning, Monique."

She waved and squeezed through the crowd. I tried to stop thinking about Monique and tried to plan my outfit for tonight. I had twenty minutes to shower and dress before Amir came to pick me up. Good thing my hair was laid already.

Amir was waiting on Tilly's stoop when I got off the train. So much for the twenty minutes I had left to get ready. For a moment I considered going on the date just as I was, but I needed to put on more deodorant and had no makeup on at all. That wasn't going to work.

"Hey, NaTasha, what's going on?" Amir said. He had on dark slacks and a light blue polo shirt, a nice change from the white apron and khakis that I usually saw him in. He was leaning against the door with one foot crossed over the other. He looked more like a model than my date. My heart started to beat fast and my palms got really wet.

"Hey, Amir, I'm just getting back," I told him. I didn't know what else to say. Only five minutes in and I was already saying stupid things. "You want to come up while I get ready?"

Tilly would flip out if she knew I had a boy in her apartment all by myself without her being there.

"Sure," he said, following me up the stairs.

My whole body rose in temperature. I pointed to the couch I usually slept on so Amir could sit down and relax while I went to get ready. I scanned the area for any of my panties or bras lying around but didn't see any.

"So, get comfortable and I'll be right back," I said. "Can I get you anything?"

He shook his head no and smiled. "Only you."

Amir was sitting in my living room and I was about to take my clothes off. If Tilly walked in now, she would have a heart attack. I stripped and jumped into the shower, lathering myself two extra times. I brushed, flossed, and gargled with mouthwash. I dressed quickly, but slow enough so I wouldn't start sweating, and applied two layers of lip gloss. When I walked out of the bathroom, Amir whistled.

"Wow, you look great, NaTasha," he said, standing to his feet. He put down the magazine he was reading and gave me a once-over. I could see his eyes tracing the bottom of my jean skirt.

"Thanks, you too," I said. I snatched my purse from the floor and headed for the door. "So, what movie are we seeing?"

I moved to the door expecting Amir to follow me. He didn't, and instead sat back down on the couch. When he saw me looking at him, he patted the seat on the couch next to him.

"We're late for the movie already, so I thought we could just stay here," he said.

Staying in wasn't what I had in mind. Staying in didn't require all the extra bathroom time, the extra lip gloss and perfume. Tilly wouldn't approve of us staying in her place alone.

I shook my head no and kept moving toward the door. Amir pretended not to see me and fiddled with something on his shirt. All of a sudden I felt childish and silly. Tilly trusted Amir. They had been friends for a while. She wouldn't mind. She would come home soon anyway.

I hung my purse on the doorknob and went and sat down on the chair across from Amir. He looked up and smiled at me.

"So, we staying in?" he asked with a huge grin, one spread wide across his mouth like he'd just won a bet.

"Yeah, staying in is okay," I told him, trying to sound like I wasn't disappointed with the arrangement. It was still good to be hanging out with Amir. He looked good and smelled even better. He had the best smile on a guy I'd ever seen. So what if we weren't going out for a date. I couldn't stare into his big brown eyes in a dark theater anyway. "But Tilly will probably be home soon."

"No problem, your grandmother is cool," he said, reaching for a magazine in Tilly's endless supply of reading materials. He opened the *Essence* and flipped through quickly. I looked at the door, hoping Tilly would come waddling through it, but she didn't. Amir was still flipping through the pages, not appearing to be reading anything in particular. Eventually, he looked up and put the magazine on his lap. "So, what are we going to do?"

I shrugged my shoulders. He was the one who asked me out. He was supposed to have the itinerary taken care of. Now that I had to improvise, I was at a loss. Tilly would know how to improvise. Her guests were usually entertained by a meal, good conversation, or just watching a television show.

Going out to the movie theater was looking better as the time went by.

"Did I hear something about you being a dancer?" Amir asked, in a tone clearly teasing me. Tilly had a big mouth and she was definitely the only one who would have passed that information on. Surprising, since I thought she hated my dancing. "Yep, I'm pretty sure that's what I heard. Why don't you teach me some of your moves?"

He motioned toward the area in between us near the coffee table and laughed. I didn't think so. I was going to have to think of something quick, because I definitely wasn't putting on any kind of dance show, or any other show. I crossed my legs when I saw him staring at my skirt. Automatically, I covered the scar on my knee with my hands. The fall happened ten years ago, but I still didn't like anyone staring at it. I scoured all the contents of Tilly's living room with my eyes, before remembering a deck of cards I'd seen in one of her kitchen drawers.

"Want something to drink?" I asked, changing the subject.

"Sure, thanks," he said, leaning forward and putting on a pouty face. "Does this mean no dance?"

I giggled and hurried into the kitchen. This couldn't be how all dates went. If so, I didn't know many girls who would bother. I was looking forward to Tilly coming home more than I was to spending time with Amir.

But I was stuck, so I pulled two glasses from the cabinet and poured pink lemonade into them. The ice cubes rattled in my shaky hands as I dropped them into the glasses. I opened every drawer in Tilly's kitchen searching for the playing cards.

I found them in the last drawer I looked in and carried the cards and glasses back into the living room. Amir's hand brushed mine as he took the glass from me. He didn't move his hand away.

"Thanks," he said. His fingers felt like knife blades teasing the hairs on my own hands. I didn't like it.

"You're welcome," I said, pulling my hand away from his and holding up the cards in front of us. I held them out so he'd reach for them. He took the bait but I was too quick for him.

I tried to set up every game that I knew of: Spades, Speed, War, and even Go Fish. None of them interested Amir unless we were touching in some way or another. His touch was different from our day in the park.

"NaTasha, why don't you come sit over here?" he said after the third round of War. I shrugged and moved so I was next to him on the couch. But I didn't feel entirely comfortable about it and I checked the door, praying for Tilly to walk in.

"Now it'll be harder for you to beat me," I pointed out nervously, motioning to the small distance in between us, clearly not conducive for card playing.

It was his turn to shrug and move closer to me. He threw his cards down, ending the game.

"Then I guess we'll just have to do something else." He leaned in and kissed me, pushing his tongue into my mouth. It was supposed to be nice, but it was so unexpected. I gasped for air and tried to push him away. He got the point, but dove back at my face like I was a sweet dessert he wanted to taste. I tried to keep up with him, but I couldn't. I started to get more nervous.

"Amir, wait a minute," I said, catching my breath so I wouldn't suffocate from his sucking all my available air.

"What's the problem, NaTasha?" he asked, like I'd interrupted some important business he had to attend to. "I thought you liked me."

He looked genuinely confused. He was right. I did like him and here we were all alone. It should have been nice, but this was uncomfortable. I thought of all the talks Heather and I had imagining our first dates, the ones where the guy brings a bouquet of fresh flowers, candles were lit all over the room, a romantic dinner out on the town, soft music playing in the background. There was music playing, but there was nothing romantic about this date at all.

"I do like you, I just don't like you attacking my face," I said, trying to lighten the mood. Amir didn't find any humor in the situation at all. He took a drink from the third glass of pink lemonade I'd poured him and cleared his throat.

"So, do you like me or not?" he asked, sounding like a different person. His voice was dark and harsh, almost intimidating and not friendly in the least bit.

This guy frowning at me in Tilly's living room couldn't be the same Amir from the bodega. I thought about how he joked and flirted with Tilly at the meat counter. Tilly would be so disappointed, with Amir and with me. I could almost see her standing over me yelling, "Girl, keep your morals intact."

"Yes, I do like you. Weren't we having a good time?" I asked. He nodded his head yes and leaned into me again. I did want him to like me. Heather wouldn't believe it when I told her about my real first date. Of course, I'd have to exaggerate a little, but there was music playing in the room and an old bouquet of flowers that Tilly and I had picked up after church on Sunday.

He pushed me back so I was almost lying on the sofa. Amir's body was heavy and his breathing was heavy, too. His hands wandered under my skirt. I pushed his hands away and tried really hard not to laugh when he touched me around my armpits. He kissed my neck and lifted my skirt with both hands. I thought about my pink panties right away, the ones I only wore on Mondays because of the MONDAY embroidered on the front. I wondered if Amir could see the letters. When his hands reached my thighs, Tilly's face popped into my mind again. I tried not to think about her at that moment, but she was pushing her way through my thoughts like an athlete pushing her way through a crowd in a long-distance race, both her hands raised above her head, and she was screaming, "Make sure you can face yourself in the mirror in the morning."

Tilly always said that when I was trying to make a tough decision.

I started to wiggle away from Amir and Tilly's thoughts. Neither one was easy to do. Amir's body was heavy and he kept right on kissing me and pulling at my clothing like I wasn't even there. Three buttons popped open on my shirt.

"Amir, Tilly will be back any minute," I said, gasping for air and energy to get him off of me. He ignored me at first and then mumbled something about not worrying. He must have forgotten who we were talking about. If Tilly walked in on us, Amir wouldn't be able to walk home and she would send me home in casts, too. I used my knee and pushed into his stomach until he moved. "We can't do this, Tilly will be back soon."

Amir sucked his teeth and rolled his eyes like I'd just insulted him. He brushed and straightened his clothes quickly and stood up. I pushed my skirt back down and followed him to the door. I buttoned my shirt as far up as I could. I didn't want Amir to think I didn't like him.

"I guess I was wrong about you, NaTasha," Amir said, just as he swung the door open, right in Tilly's face.

"Well, excuse me, young man," Tilly said, slamming her hands on her hips almost as hard as Amir had swung the door. Each one looked as mad as the other, for very different reasons. My heart was racing. "And just what were you wrong about in regards to NaTasha?"

Amir's face softened a little, but he still didn't give up much information. He muttered something that sounded like, "Sorry, Ms. Tilly," and pushed past her. Tilly kept the scowl on her face and hands molded at her hips until he was out of sight. The only things we heard were his footsteps taking the stairs two at a time all the way to floor one. For a second I thought Tilly was going to chase after him, but she didn't.

"So, what in the Lord's name happened up in here tonight?" Tilly asked me. I really wasn't in the mood for her questions. I turned to walk away but remembered first who I was dealing with.

"Excuse you?" she said.

"Tilly, it was nothing," I said, knowing I couldn't tell her the details of the story without embarrassing myself and making her angrier than she already was. I was going to have to figure out something to tell her, though. She already knew something wasn't right in her home.

"Nothing my big backside," she said, walking into the apartment. She took off her sweater and hung it behind the door, where my purse was hanging, then turned to face me. She scanned my wrinkled clothing.

"Did something . . . happen?" she asked, making her sex face, the one where one eyebrow goes up and the other way down. "Because if he hurt you, I'll just have to kill him."

"No, Tilly, it wasn't like that at all," I told her. I covered my eyes and put my head in my hands. It had been a long day for us both. I didn't feel like reliving what happened with Amir.

"Then exactly how was it, Miss Thang?" she asked, enunciating every word slowly and deliberately. She was getting more annoyed by the moment. Her shoulders were hunched a little and she heaved in and out with great effort. She took a step closer to me and raised both eyebrows. "Well?"

"I can still look myself in the eye in the morning," I told her.

Tilly's facial expression changed right away. She was still angry, but proud and surprised, too. She nodded her head and kissed me on the forehead.

"You okay?" she asked.

"Yeah, I'm okay," I answered. I really was okay. I was glad she had come home when she did, though. I could tell she was, too. She fiddled around in the kitchen for a few minutes, but every few minutes, she'd peek out and look at me.

"You know I love you, right, girl?" Tilly finally asked after checking on me a million and one times. I was still sitting in the same spot.

"Yeah, I know, Tilly," I said.

She nodded and went back to opening and closing drawers in the kitchen. Something told me we wouldn't be shopping at the corner bodega anymore. After what felt like hours of sitting inside with Tilly pacing, I needed some air. I promised her I wouldn't leave the stoop. She reluctantly let me go, even though I knew she'd be watching from the window upstairs.

"You be back up here soon, you hear me?" Tilly called.

"I promise," I told her.

I changed my shirt and grabbed my cell. When I got downstairs, Khalik was there bouncing his basketball.

"Why are you always hitting that stupid ball?" I asked him, rolling my eyes at him. He smiled and bounced it over to me.

I caught it with both arms, sat down, and tossed it back. There was something about Khalik's smile and calm demeanor that always made me feel better.

We passed the ball back and forth for a few minutes in silence. Every time I threw it back with more and more force, letting all of my disappointment and anger leave with every toss. He didn't go easy on me, either. He kept smiling and pushed the ball back to me just as hard. We kept at it until the ball sailed past me and we were both laughing hysterically.

When we regained our composure, we sat in silence for a few minutes.

"I told you to stay away from that dude," Khalik said after awhile. Not rudely, just in a matter-of-fact way. He was right, he had told me, and I just didn't listen.

"Yeah, you did," I said, not looking at him. We had a full conversation without really saying much. He wasn't there to judge me or tease, he was just there. And I was glad. Right at that moment he was the only one I would have wanted to be with. I shoved him lightly with my shoulder. I wanted to sit there with Khalik all night.

CHAPTER
NINETEEN

THE PHONE WAS ringing as I walked into the apartment.
I ran to answer before the voice mail kicked in. Everyone
knew not to call my grandmother's house after nine o'clock.
Even though she may be awake sometimes, Tilly thought it
was rude.

"Hello?"

My mom was awfully chipper on the other line. She
sounded like she was having a party at the house. I told
her so.

"Of course I miss you, honey, but I'm glad you're getting along so well with Tilly," she said. "I'm really proud
of you. Really, I expected you to quit a long time ago. We
all did."

I wanted to ask her who all the people were who thought I
would have quit.

"Thanks a lot," I said. My dad joined us on another phone.

"How's my little girl doing in the big city?" he asked.

"I'm okay, Dad," I said. "I'm glad I decided to stick it out.
There were things for me to learn here, but I can't talk too

much about it because nosy Tilly will overhear and make me tell her how right she was over and over."

My parents and I laughed. I was proud of me, too, for staying and seeing this experience through. I missed home and my best friend, but the kids in New York weren't as bad as I thought they'd be. Getting through Quiana, Rochelle, and Monique was rough, but they had good sides like everyone else.

"Why are you guys calling so late anyway?" I asked. They knew the no-calls-after-nine rule better than me. In fact, they taught it to me. "You are coming up to see the recognition ceremony on Thursday, aren't you?"

"Of course, we'll be there," they said together. "We have a surprise for you and thought you'd want to know right away."

"Well, what is it?" I asked. I was more scared than excited, but I didn't think they could tell.

"Heather is going to come up with us," my dad said, in an announcer's voice, like I'd just won the lottery or something.

"Oh," I said. My parents probably didn't know how my best friend Heather found a new best friend while I was away. They probably also didn't know that my new friends wouldn't be thrilled at all to see my old best friend, especially since I wasn't sure I even wanted to see her yet. "I mean, that's great. I'm sure the girls at Amber's Place will be really happy, too . . . the more the merrier."

"Well, okay," my mom said, sounding a little confused. The thought of bringing my two worlds together made me more uneasy than I had felt in a long time. I could just picture the faces of the girls at the center.

"It's just that I've worked hard to get to know the girls up here and I don't think Heather will understand that," I told them. A week ago I would have jumped at the chance to get away from Quiana and to spend time with Heather.

"Well, hang on a minute now and I guess you girls can talk about that and work it out amongst yourselves," my dad said. He said good-bye to me and I could hear the phone being passed to someone else.

"Hey, Tash, I miss you," Heather said. Her voice sounded different, a little whiny and unreal.

"Yeah, me too," I said.

"Are you surprised?" she asked, trying to sound excited. She sounded as excited as I was trying to be. I nodded my head yes and waited for her to finish telling me all the outfits she'd bought for the trip. Already, my head was spinning. "I started to invite Stephanie to come along, too."

"But you didn't, right?" I didn't know what I was more upset about, having my best friend invade my new friends, or the mention that my best friend was thinking about bringing my enemy along with her.

"Don't worry, Tash, she may not be able to come anyway," Heather said.

"I can't believe you would do that," I told her.

I had no more words. It would either be a great trip or a disaster. I would just have to wait and see. The girls in the Bronx had a hard enough time adjusting to me, let alone Heather and Stephanie. That was a completely different story. Heather definitely wouldn't understand anything about the girls or their lives. And the girls really would think I was a sellout after meeting Heather and Stephanie.

The call waiting beeped.

"Look, Heather, I'll see you soon, but I've got to answer this," I told her.

"Fine," she said, disappointed. "You know, Tash, you even sound different. I feel like I don't know who you are anymore."

"Well, that makes two of us," I said, clicking over to the other line.

"Hey, Sellout, big news." Quiana was on the other line. She sounded like she was out of breath.

"What's up? Is it Monique?" I asked.

"No, Monique's fine," she said. "I just thought you and Tilly would want to hear about Maria and the baby. She had a girl. Her cousin just called here."

"That's great news," I said excitedly. "How is she? What did she name the baby? Is she okay to have visitors?"

"Slow down, crazy," Quiana said, in her monotone, tough girl voice. Somewhere deep down, I knew she was excited about the baby, too. She had called, after all. "I don't know all that, but I'm sure Red will tell us when we get in tomorrow."

"Okay," I said. "Thanks for calling, Quiana."

"Don't mention it," she said, "to anyone."

Quiana didn't want anyone to know she had called me. I

assured her I wouldn't mention it again, and hung up the phone.

There was so much going on in my head, there was no way I could rest well before the biggest event of my life. My two worlds were meeting and all I could see was a recipe for disaster.

CHAPTER TWENTY

MY CHECKLIST WAS almost complete. It was amazing the difference a couple of weeks made at Amber's Place. The girls really came through. Tuesday and Wednesday were spent in a whirlwind of activity as all the girls worked hard to get everything done for the big day.

Quiana and Red were going over the programs for the reception when I walked into the room on Thursday morning. I was shocked that Quiana had beaten me to Amber's Place. She was working alongside Red and had the printed certificates in her hand.

She saw the confused look on my face.

"What?" Quiana snapped, dropping the programs and the certificates that she had been holding on the table. I smiled at Red. Quiana looked angry and leaned back forcefully in her chair. I sat down next to her and picked up one of the programs.

"So, what do you think, NaTasha?" Red asked, grinning from ear to ear. She was proud of us. In a lot of ways, these girls were her children, even me. She'd trusted us with this project and we'd done a great job. But I couldn't have done it without the help of each of the girls, including Quiana. I told Red so. "I have to say, girls," Red told us, "I'm impressed. I didn't expect you to work together, let alone put together a program as nice as this one. Your family and friends are going to be so proud."

Quiana stared at the door every few minutes and checked her watch, too. She wasn't waiting for her family members; she already said that no one was coming to see her. Susan and Shaunda walked through the door chatting excitedly. Rochelle walked in next. Quiana nodded to her, but kept her arms crossed and her teeth clenched.

Red updated the girls with the latest news about the reception, but kept a close watch on the time. Only a handful of hours were left and we still had to decorate and run through the program. Monique was late.

We chatted about the last-minute details as long as possible, but everyone was thinking the same thing. Where was Monique?

"So, ladies, let's get started," Red said, glancing at the door one last time. She looked disappointed and worried. "We need to decorate and rehearse. What would you like to do first?"

"Let's decorate and get it over with," Rochelle said, jumping up with a bag of streamers and balloons in her hand. She started handing streamers to each of us and pointing us toward the tables in the reception hall.

After an hour of taping streamers to tables and arranging flower bouquets, I couldn't concentrate anymore. I dropped the paper plates and plastic silverware onto the table of drinks and reached for my cell phone to leave yet another voice mail message on Monique's phone.

"I just called her, too," Quiana said, coming up next to me. She was holding her phone in one hand and a stack of programs in the other hand. Quiana shrugged her shoulders and shook her head. "You can try, though, just in case."

While I called, Quiana dropped off the flyers with Rochelle and went to wait for Monique by the door. Rochelle tried to hand her another bag of streamers, but Quiana blew her off.

I left another message and went to get my next assignment. Rochelle hesitantly threw me a bag of purple and silver curtains to wrap around the podium and stage area.

"Pretty soon she's going to go after her," I told her, motioning toward Quiana at the doorway.

"Yeah, I know," Rochelle answered quickly.

"You two are good friends, have you heard anything from her?" I asked. Even if she had heard, I wasn't sure Rochelle would tell me anything, but there was a chance.

"No, I haven't heard anything, and what's it to you?" Rochelle said, folding an extra tablecloth.

"I was just asking, because I thought you'd be concerned, too," I told her.

"I am concerned, but I can't drop my life every time Monique decides to go back to that loser, now can I?" she said, snapping at me without stopping her work. She wiped out the inside of a punch bowl and set it back in place next to a stack of plastic cups. She sounded harsh and I think she realized it after I stood there for a few minutes in silence. She continued in a softer voice, "I've done that before and I told her I wasn't doing it no more. This time she'll have to learn on her own."

This wasn't Monique's first disappearing act. Quiana looked like she was waiting for permission to leave. I didn't blame her at all. If Heather ever went missing, I wouldn't know what to do.

Thinking about Heather made me a little sad. Our last few conversations hadn't gone so well. Maybe she wasn't my best friend anymore at all. I wouldn't be surprised now if she didn't come with my folks for the ceremony.

Red placed six candles in the center of each table, representing each girl being recognized at the reception.

"I really am proud of the work you girls have done for the center," Red said, "and I want you to know you're always welcome to come and visit us anytime."

"Not a chance, Red," Rochelle joked. We all laughed.

"Well, let's at least practice our program for tonight before you all tear out of here," she said.

I whispered into Red's ear, and Red turned to look at Quiana and nodded. I grabbed my purse and sweater and took Quiana by the arm. She jumped away from me and put up her fists. I held up my hands in surrender and smiled at her.

"Let's go," I told her.

"Wait, girls . . ." Red yelled after us. We turned. "What about gifts for everyone?"

"You let us worry about that," I told her. "We already have something in mind."

"We do?" Quiana asked. I nodded and pulled her the rest of the way down the hallway. Once outside she finally shook away from me.

"Sellout, where are we going?" She enunciated every syllable like Tilly does when she scolded me for something.

"You want to find Monique, right?" I challenged her. She didn't say anything, just got this blank look on her face. I took that as a yes. "Well, let's go see if she's okay. Let's go find her."

I didn't wait for her to respond. I knew she wanted to find Monique as much as I did. I turned and walked up the block to the train. Quiana followed a close distance behind me.

"Fine, but this isn't the way," she said, grabbing me before I stepped onto a downtown-bound train.

"I know," I answered, pulling her into the fully packed car. "We have a stop to make first."

She gave me a look, but continued to follow my lead. I'd expected her to put up more of a fight than she did, but I guess she was tired of arguing with me. I'm sure she was thinking the sooner we found Monique and got through the reception, the better. I couldn't agree with her more.

We got to Tilly's block about thirty minutes later.

"Where are we going?" Quiana asked me. Pretty soon, if I didn't tell her where we were headed, she could turn around and leave me on my own.

"This is Tilly's block," I said proudly, like I was giving a celebrity home tour to a visitor. I waved my arms dramatically and pointed out Tilly's building, the old movie theater, and the bodega. I looked back at her and smiled. She wasn't amused. I dropped my arms to my side. "We're just picking up someone who may be able to help and then we can be on our way."

She nodded and followed me to the basketball courts and right to the person I was looking for. Khalik was standing alone against a fence, bouncing his basketball and juggling his cell phone in the other hand.

"Ooh, you're so talented," I said, teasing him. "You know, that ball is not a good look for you all the time."

Quiana stood next to me and eyeballed Khalik. He looked at her, nodded, and then snapped the phone shut and rolled his eyes at me.

"What do you care?" he snapped back playfully.

He bounce-passed the ball and squared his body in front of me. His eyes focused on me, challenging me to play with him. I could hear Quiana huffing impatiently next to me. There would be plenty of time later to play with Khalik. I caught the ball with both hands and held it against my right hip. He eyed the ball like it was a hamburger he was dying to bite into. I snapped my fingers in front of his face to get his attention again.

"Not now," I said, tossing the ball back to him. A few of the other guys on the court had drifted closer to us. Khalik had handsome friends. Quiana kept her eyes on all of them, like a protective watchdog. "I, I mean, *we* need your help for a little while."

"Oh, yeah, the way I see it you and your girl need a lot more help than you think if that's the way you always handle the ball," he said, slapping high five with an oddly tall kid standing next to him. They laughed. Quiana sucked her teeth and elbowed me in the arm. I had two seconds to enlist Khalik or she was out of there.

"Not with basketball, stupid," I said. "I need you to come with us now and help me out with something . . . and you may want to bring a few of your friends."

Khalik smiled wider than I had ever seen him smile. His friends, who had deserted their game on the court to listen in on our conversation, started hooting and hollering and shoving one another around like Quiana and I were volunteering for a kissing booth and they were in line waiting for a turn. I rolled my eyes and pointed to the court exit. I couldn't tell how many guys were following along with Khalik, but I didn't care. When we found Monique, if we found her, the more help the better, especially because we didn't know what, or who, to expect when we found her.

"What do we need them for?" Quiana hissed, as we swiped our subway cards through once again. A few of Khalik's friends skipped swiping their cards, and jumped over the turnstiles instead. Maybe it was a mistake to have invited all of them. I shrugged at Quiana. I didn't know if we needed them at all, I just felt better having them come along just in case.

"Monique may be in trouble when we find her," I said quietly. "I'm not sure, but these guys may be able to help us."

Quiana looked at me and didn't speak. I think we were both taking in the gravity of what I had just told her. I knew she was replaying the conversation with Monique in her head, because I was, too. Monique had promised she'd be okay and at Amber's Place early to decorate. She wasn't the type to go back on her word.

Quiana and I watched the boys goof-off on the train. Two of them hung from the handlebars to have a pull-up competition, right there in front of other passengers. A few others cheered them on. Khalik sat quietly across from us throwing his ball from one hand to the other. He studied my face deeply, as if he could tell I was worried about something. I hadn't explained it all yet, but I was glad he knew I was no longer joking around.

The train rattled along loudly. The boys finally tired of the handlebars games and took seats next to us. As we got closer to Monique's stop, my heart began to race unsteadily. Even as I prayed for her safety, I could feel we were stepping into some kind of danger. I worried about what I was getting myself— and all of us—into.

The train stopped at Kingsbridge Road in the Bronx and Quiana and I led the way out of the station. The boys followed behind us like a college football team ready to win a bowl game.

While Quiana led the way, I filled Khalik in on the story about Monique, and he understood immediately why I'd come to get him.

"You talked to her, right?" he asked, putting a plan of action together in his head. I nodded and followed Quiana down a well-lit alley between a small grocery and a liquor store. "Then I'm sure she's cool."

Quiana made a left turn at a dead-end street, right in front of a housing project. She pointed to one of the buildings and motioned for me and Khalik to follow. Khalik whispered something to some of his friends, who jumped into action like a presidential security team. They stood guard under street-lights and next to trees all the way to the end of the block. Khalik took my hand and we walked next to Quiana into one of the brick buildings.

CHAPTER TWENTY-ONE

BEFORE WE EVEN got to the door to the apartment, we heard loud music wafting down the hallway toward us. When we first knocked, Loser Boyfriend opened it only a crack. When I asked for Monique, he started to close the door again. When he saw Khalik standing behind us, he changed his mind.

"What up, cuz?" L.B. yelled loudly, grabbing Khalik's outstretched hand and half hugging him, patting him roughly on the back.

"Everything is everything, playa," Khalik answered. L.B. pulled Khalik into the apartment and had almost forgotten about Quiana and me in the hallway. "Oh, my girls here wanted to holler at Mo. She around?"

We had all eyed him and he us. He had pulled at his sagging sweatpants and dropped himself into a shabby green recliner that didn't recline. He pointed the remote control in his hand to a stereo next to the baseball game on his TV and motioned toward a closed door down the hall. We let the door slam behind us and shuffled quickly toward Monique. For the first time, Quiana even looked uncomfortable.

We found Monique huddled in the corner of her bedroom. She was rifling through photographs and crying at the same time. There were children in tattered clothes and with wild, unkempt hair smiling in the pictures. Maybe they were Monique's siblings. By the way she held the pictures and cried a little more at each one, she clearly kept them somewhere deep in her heart.

Monique hardly noticed Quiana and me enter her bedroom, which surprised me because of the small amount of space around us. We barely fit around a pile of unfolded clothes and a twin mattress pushed up against one wall and the window. A red and white striped bedsheet was half tucked under the mattress, but didn't fit all the way across. The other matching bedsheet hung over the window guards like a curtain. It blew back and forth slightly in the wind.

"Mo, what happened, girl?" Quiana asked. She knelt down on top of the pile of clothes so she was facing Monique. No answer. Monique didn't look up or move a muscle. After a few minutes she flipped to another photo and started crying again. "We waited for you all morning. You didn't hear your phone ringing?"

Quiana rifled through the clothes under her and the photos lying around Monique, looking for a phone. She didn't find one. Quiana shifted uncomfortably and shook her head back and forth. The silence was starting to bother me. Monique had to know how much trouble it was leaving Amber's Place to come find her, not to mention how much trouble I'd be in if Tilly knew where I was and what I had gotten involved in.

"Yeah, Monique, we were really worried about you," I said. I took a seat on the mattress and held my bag in my lap. "Weren't you planning to be recognized at the reception tonight?"

I knew from walking in and seeing her sitting in the corner crying that she probably wasn't concerned with the reception. That was the least of her worries, especially with L.B. in the other room on the couch.

"Enough with the tired pictures already," Quiana snapped. Monique and I both jumped. The pictures flew out of Monique's hands and fell into the pile of clothing between the girls. I stared back and forth to see who would move first. "You know I hate that dude. Why you have us come up here looking for you? You could have called."

Quiana lectured her like a child. I felt sorry for Monique, for more than just getting yelled at. I wondered if Khalik was alright in the living room. I could still hear loud music playing. I prayed the screams I heard were coming from a song and not from him signaling for help.

"And you could at least have the decency to look at us," Quiana shot out. She pulled Monique's chin from its hiding place against her neck. That's when we saw the mushy dark skin swelling around her right eye, the wound she'd been hiding in tissues since we'd walked in her room.

"Oh my God, Monique," I tossed my purse aside on the bed and rushed toward her. Quiana put her hand up like a stop sign right in front of my chest.

"No, pack a bag for her," Quiana said. Her voice was steady. She was in total control and gave orders like a seasoned drill sergeant. I was glad, too, because I was so shook up I didn't know what to do. "There's a bag over by the closet, fill it."

I did as I was told. I tried to color coordinate, but it was hard to concentrate. Behind my back I could hear Quiana helping Monique to her feet. She changed her clothes, washed and made up her face, and brushed her hair. Only up close could you still see the marks.

My mind raced as I filled her pink duffel to the brim. What would Quiana do to L.B. now? What would he do to us? How would Red and Tilly react? Why was Monique putting up with this? Where were her parents? What were Khalik's friends doing downstairs? Were they wondering what was taking us so long? What outfit should Monique wear for the reception? Why was I thinking about Monique's attire? Would any man ever hit me like that? No, Tilly would kill him with a pair of her cooking shears. I picked a pair of small black ballet slippers and zipped the duffel shut.

"You okay, Monique?" I asked her. I knew it was the wrong question to ask her, but I didn't know what else to say. She nodded. I slung my purse and her bag over my shoulder and stood next to them.

Quiana had combed Monique's hair so her bangs swept just right across her bruised eye. She did look much better, but she was a little hunched over and stuck closely behind Quiana. Quiana's anger hadn't subsided. She stood in front of Monique like a momma lion protecting her young. Only a young naïve animal would attempt to get at that cub. I didn't even think L.B. was that stupid. We walked past him without a word.

"Alright, man, you stay up," Khalik said behind us. He was at the door right as I was walking through it. I could tell by how quickly he jumped up that he'd been ready to go for a while. He shut the door behind him before L.B. could even respond. The echo of the door slamming reverberated in my head all the way out of the building and down the street.

"Let's roll," Khalik called, motioning for all his friends to join us. They appeared around us like weeds in uncut grass from their hiding corners.

"We got two hours until the reception, one to find gifts and one to get back. Are we going to make it?" I asked. I looked at Quiana and Monique and they both looked back at me, one with confidence and the other blankly. "Yeah, we're going to make it," I decided.

We walked to the train station as quickly as Monique could shuffle her feet.

CHAPTER TWENTY-TWO

QUIANA AND I piled into the reception hall with our entourage. The reception hall looked considerably different with all of our friends and family gathered around the decor we had worked so hard arranging. I spotted my parents and Tilly and waved.

Heather and Stephanie waved like they were family, distant cousins who I wasn't thrilled to have to spend time with. I waved back. Quiana pushed me forward and we continued walking to the front of the audience toward our seats. I nodded and turned toward the front of the stage.

"What's the deal?" Quiana asked me as we settled in. I glanced back at Heather and Stephanie, who were still staring at me, and shook my head to let Quiana know everything was okay, and to convince myself to let it go.

"Just saw some old friends, that's all," I told her and took my seat next to Susan. The other girls from Amber's Place were seated all together in the front three rows. Tilly, Red, and Coach were seated like royalty on the stage, facing the audience. Tilly wore a black Sunday church suit and matching hat, Coach a Sean John tracksuit, and Red a dark blue business suit with a bright orange scarf draped around her neck. Red stepped up to the podium to begin.

"Welcome, everyone, and thank you for coming to celebrate all of these special girls," Red said, as she shifted from one foot to the other behind the podium. "Girls come to Amber's Place for various reasons, but no matter the reason, they all mean the world to us. I'd like to take a moment to recognize these girls."

Red named each of the girls, me included, slowly, as if giving the audience time to reflect on our lives and our accomplishments. This was enough to put Susan over the edge. I saw tears after each name. Red smiled and pointed us out one by one, some names drawing thunderous applause and chants like at an awards show on TV.

"Okay, the moment we've all been waiting for . . . all of these girls have grown since they've been at Amber's Place, but some more than others," Red said, motioning for Tilly to join her up at the podium.

Tilly loved center stage so she took her time, waiting for the applause for her to grow and then die down a bit. I clapped, too. Everyone in the room knew Tilly and loved her just as much as I did.

"And let the church say amen," Tilly yelled into the mic. The crowd went wild with laughter. I knew someone would have to drag Tilly off the stage if she started preaching. "Just kidding, I won't be long, but these girls know I don't start nothing without giving God the praise."

She motioned for us all to clap for our maker just like a congregation does in church. No one was surprised and we followed her lead.

"Now we can begin," she said dramatically. "I love all these girls just like they were my own. Every last one of them could tell you a story that would make you lose your lunch and then cry like a baby. Today, I wanted someone to speak who had worked like a dog to better herself and really make a change around here. She's helped me whenever I needed it and recently helped my own granddaughter when she had a hard time coming to the center. Shaunda, get on up here and tell these folks how you made it."

I thought I would choke when Tilly called me out like that, but I was also proud of Shaunda, who was walking slowly up to the podium. This was her moment. The girls had to listen to her now. Now everyone would see her. She hugged Tilly and Red, and gave Coach a high five on her way over to the microphone.

Shaunda wore a blue baby doll dress with the collar raised and a matching hair tie holding her ponytail together. She looked more ready for a photo shoot than a reception speech. I could just hear my mom and Tilly complimenting her on her first impression outfit later on. She leaned in too close to the mic, almost like she was going to kiss it, and started in a whisper.

I leaned forward and so did a few others around me. I saw her mouth moving but no words came out. Coach jumped up and pretended to adjust the mic and gave our speaker an encouraging pat on the back. Shaunda cleared her throat and started again.

Quiana had a slight smirk on her face and started rubbing imaginary dirt from under her fingernails.

Shaunda looked past us to someone in the back of the room. She nodded, straightened her stance, and spoke directly into the microphone, commanding our attention. I looked back to see Rex, who was wearing a slightly tattered brown business suit with a yellow pocket square and yellow and black checkered tie. With his new haircut and sans shopping cart, I almost didn't recognize him. He winked at me and turned his attention back to his assignment.

"When I came to Amber's Place, I wasn't surprised at what I'd found, girls just like me who needed a place to go, who didn't accept me. I came in the first day to meet Red and Tilly, who convinced me that my life could be different if I wanted it to be, but knowing my life would be just the same as it's always been, with people judging me, not liking me, making fun of me, and harassing me. I was almost convinced at first, but every time I came back, things only got worse. In elementary school the white kids didn't like me because I was a tall black girl who wasn't quite like them. The black kids my age wouldn't associate with me because my skin was too light. I didn't talk like them and I had one white friend, who was an outcast, too. For a long time I tried to vary my hairstyle, choose new clothes, adjust how I pronounced my words. I even wiped skin bleach across my face and arms, hoping and praying my caramel color would fade overnight so I'd have more friends, more chance of fitting in. I tried everything I knew to try, and everything I saw my classmates doing around me, just trying to be liked."

As Shaunda spoke, I could feel my body temperature start to rise. I shifted in my seat and folded and unfolded my legs a few times. The girls around me listened to Shaunda intently, as if she were a life coach handing out free survival tips. I wanted to listen, too, but it was hard for me to hear her story. Shaunda may not have realized it, but she was telling my story, too.

I certainly didn't want perfect strangers knowing the truth. I felt like the whole crowd could see right through me and I wasn't even the one onstage.

"I was by myself a lot of the time. When people were around, I told them whatever they wanted to hear. If my mom wanted me to talk, I talked. If she wanted me to listen, I listened. If she needed an explanation, I gave her one. She knew everything about me, except for how unhappy I really was. Neither of my parents had ever seen the marks on my skin before. I started hurting myself back in elementary school and no one had ever noticed. Or so I thought. I knew better than to lie to my mother, but keeping a secret was different. She found out most things on her own, like when I changed my voice to sound like my friends, or when I cut the heads off of all of the black professionals' posters my mother had taped to my walls to replace them with lighter, and sometimes whiter, faces. My teachers and parents finally started noticing that I was crying every day about things they couldn't understand.

During class I wasn't paying attention and used any excuse I could think of to leave the room and head for the bathroom. I was failing every subject in school because I couldn't focus. That got my parents' attention, but by then it was too late. It got to the point where I ate alone, I cried alone, and I almost disappeared completely. I felt like I was literally in a world all by myself. So, finally, one day I decided to give up even trying."

I snuck a look behind me. My parents and Heather were right in my line of sight. I couldn't tell what they were thinking. My mother's eyebrows were raised and arched, like they do when she tells me, "I told you so." I slinked back around and prayed Shaunda would wrap up her speech sooner rather than later.

"One day my guidance counselor called my parents and me into a meeting about my behavior. She told us she was disturbed and confused at what was going on with me and how anxious she was to find a solution for me and for all parties involved. The counselor very strongly suggested I come to Amber's Place to meet Red and Tilly. She said she knew of other girls like me who needed a home away from home and that this may be the answer we had all been looking for. The counselor also told me the girls at the center would be more forgiving because they all had issues to deal with and that I would fit in better under these circumstances. Well, she was wrong. Coming here was harder than being at school, but there was something comforting about knowing that I had somewhere else to escape to when one place became too hard to deal with."

Shaunda took a long pause and looked toward us, not at anyone in particular, just over to where all the girls were seated in the first few rows. It was Quiana's turn to shift uncomfortably in her seat. Her arms were crossed now and she was staring in her lap. Monique and Rochelle looked just as uncomfortable. No one was willing to look at Shaunda anymore.

She was saying everything I had been feeling my entire life, and sometimes still felt. I had never fit in, either. Maybe none of us have. It really wasn't important to fit in with a popular group of people, but I had made it that important. All of the girls around me had made it that serious, too. I looked around me.

We talked, listened, and counted on one another and we all showed up at the center religiously. Shaunda wiped a tear away just as I felt one sliding down my own cheek.

"Then I met Red and Tilly, and with their help, I changed the way I was thinking. We all have a story. We all feel like outsiders, out of place in a world that should accept us just because. But the world doesn't accept us and instead, we fight each other. At Amber's Place I've learned to stop fighting other people and myself. I can't change other people, but I can change how I view myself. That's a power I've never known. Part of the reason I'm standing here today is because of a few ladies and my speech coach, Rex, who really listened to my story, understood my story, and cared about me. If they could all come up here with me, please, I'd like to present a few awards to them on behalf of all the girls at Amber's Place."

As the awardees joined Shaunda onstage, the rest of us composed ourselves. The parents and siblings clapped and dabbed at their eyes. I wiped my face dry with the backs of both my hands, and was shocked to see the other girls around me doing the same. As Shaunda finished up, I felt a huge weight lifting from my shoulders. She told my story, and the stories of all of the girls, better than I could have hoped.

"Red, these are for you," Shaunda said, handing Red a bag full of personalized notebooks and a new pair of hot pink sunglasses. Red slipped on the shades and modeled for the audience.

"Coach, you're next." The Amber's Place girls whistled and pretended to spike volleyballs at her. She stepped closer to Shaunda and played along with us, pretending to dodge all the balls coming her way. She unwrapped a shiny new whistle to wear around her neck and a volleyball signed by the women's USA Olympic team. Coach was touched.

"Ms. Tilly, please come forward," Shaunda said, looking at me as she spoke. "This is a gift we all thought long and hard about."

Tilly pulled a jewelry box out of her small bag and clutched her chest as if on cue. She breathed in dramatically and lifted the top of the box and screamed.

"Girl, you had better stop it," Tilly said, pulling the pearls out of the box slowly. Shaunda took the bracelet from her and closed the clasp around Tilly's wrist. Tilly spun around and around while we all clapped. She finally looked at me when she was done spinning and I winked at her. She leaned into the mic again. "I want to thank all of you out there. I'm very proud of you girls and I will be signing autographs in the back."

We all laughed and Shaunda reached for her last bag.

"And last but not least, Rex, I couldn't have done this speech today without your guidance and advice," Shaunda said, handing Rex a small bag like the others. I was pretty sure no one else in the audience knew who Rex was or what he looked like earlier in the day, but it didn't seem like anyone cared. He fiddled with the wrapping and pulled out his gift. I thought I heard a collective gasp from the crowd, waiting to see what he had in his hands.

Rex opened the engraved stopwatch slowly and showed it to us before slipping it back in the box.

"Now is a good time to change a life, right, Rex?" Shaunda asked. He nodded and slipped the watch into his pocket. We clapped and he hugged Shaunda and smiled politely. Rex looked like a proud father.

Red called each of the girls onstage one by one. I was surprised, and happy, to be included. Tilly and Coach handed out hugs and certificates. When the ceremony was over, there wasn't a dry eye in the room.

Most of the girls met up to hug their family members and smile for pictures. Quiana didn't rush to meet anyone, so I dragged her along with me. She wasn't happy about it, but she came. Tilly met up with us just as we reached my parents.

"Tilly and Tash, we're so proud of you. You put on a great show up there," my dad said, kissing us each on the forehead. "What can I say, Tilly, you were right."

"I'm sorry, Walter, I couldn't quite hear you, what was that?" Tilly said, laughing and jabbing him in his stomach and holding one hand up to her ear.

"You were right, Mom, and thank you for taking care of our little girl," my mom said, hugging Tilly and then me.

"Mom, this is Quiana," I said lightly, shoving Quiana on the shoulder. She shoved me back and nodded to my mom. "And, Quiana, this is my mom."

Heather and Stephanie walked up behind us and we exchanged awkward hellos. The moment I met up with Heather again had played so differently in my head before. I thought I would scream at her for betraying our friendship. But things were different now. I was different.

"So, does all this mean you won't be worried for your next visit with Tilly?" my mom asked jokingly. I looked at all those standing around me. I had too many reasons to come back now. They all stared at me.

"I'll be back before the girls even notice I'm gone," I said, shoving Quiana again. Everyone was smiling. "I'll be here so much they won't be able to get rid of me if they tried."

Quiana rolled her eyes and went off to grab some punch and cookies.

CHAPTER TWENTY-THREE

"OKAY, FOLKS, LET'S eat," Tilly called. The next night we were gathered in Tilly's apartment, celebrating. We'd moved all the living room furniture aside and set up a large table to make room for the guests. "Last one to the table gets to serve all the plates."

I followed my parents, Khalik, Heather, Stephanie, Quiana, Red, Ms. Rose, Monique, Rochelle, Maria, Shaunda, Coach, and Rex into Tilly's kitchen. She had overdone it with the food as usual, but I was glad, one last meal to share with her before I headed back home. It was bittersweet.

I couldn't wait to drive past the Welcome to Adams Park sign on the highway, but I was also so sad to be leaving Tilly and the few people I had come to know and care about at Amber's Place.

"Tilly, this looks fantastic, as usual," my mom said. "One day maybe I'll be able to throw down like this."

"I don't think so, girl," Tilly said sarcastically. "You'd actually have to know where a stove was kept for that to ever happen."

We all laughed. I looked around the room at all my favorite people and felt overwhelmed. For the first time in a long time, I found a place where I fit in.

Heather munched on her salad and croutons, apparently some diet she'd started at home after Marcia told her she'd been gaining too much weight. Quiana had sat next to her to taunt her with a full plate of fried chicken and mashed potatoes.

The adults chatted quietly while shoving food in their mouths at the same time. Khalik, Rex, and my dad talked sports loudly. I wanted to remember this night. I didn't want it to ever end.

I dabbled in my macaroni and cheese, but couldn't really concentrate on food. I heard the words coming from the table and the noise coming from the street, but my head was overwhelmed with all that had happened in such a short span of time.

"NaTasha, what are you thinking about over there?" my mom asked.

"Oh, nothing, I was just thinking about how great this trip has been," I said. "Tilly, you were right, this experience has changed me."

Mom and Tilly exchanged looks. Heather jumped in, even with her mouth full of tomato.

"I'm glad to have my best friend back so we can get back to ballet," she said. "I talked with Marcia about getting you back into rehearsal and she agreed, if you'll just make a few changes. Isn't that great, Tash?"

"Actually," I said, with everyone at the long table watching me, "I had a few changes of my own in mind. Ballet really isn't my thing. And I'm done trying to please everyone around me. If it's all the same to all of you, I'd prefer to just be me."

Rex started clapping and then so did everyone else. I half stood and took a bow, laughing with the group. It felt good.

"While I have everyone's attention," I said, "I want to thank my parents for encouraging me to come. And thanks to Tilly for having me and for her good advice."

"You are welcome, baby," she said, "I'm just so glad my grandbaby came to stay with me."

"Actually, I have been thinking about staying here," I said quickly. Everyone looked confused. My mom looked shocked. My dad smiled and kept eating. Heather had dropped her fork into her salad and looked close to tears. I looked at Quiana and Khalik to see their reactions. Quiana rolled her eyes. Khalik smiled. I smiled, too, and held up my hands in surrender. "But, I know I have some unfinished business to deal with back home that I can't keep hiding from."

"Well, if you change your mind, you know you're always welcome," Tilly said. "Who wants pie?"

While I bathed in Tilly's tub that night, I felt relaxed and relieved. I knew I had made the right decision to go home. Tilly knocked on the bathroom door with a bowl of ice cream in her hand and held it up to me.

"You interested?" she asked, grinning from ear to ear. She was wearing a white nightgown with red apples on it and still wore her new bracelet.

"You know I am," I said.

I met my grandmother out in the living room and she handed me a fresh bowl of mint chocolate chip. We kicked our feet up and stared out the window.

"You glad I came, Tilly?" I asked her.

"Yeah, I'm glad, baby," she said. She started humming "I Won't Turn Back, Lord" and I grinned. I closed my eyes and listened to her song.

ACKNOWLEDGMENTS

Thanks to my family for reading the earliest versions of this story and for offering your *totally unbiased* opinions. To Mom and Dad for buying that first story-writing computer game when I was a kid (eleven more to go!). To Davey, Sam, and Nate for your unwavering support, encouragement, and even the jokes. To my New School classmates and teachers for writing and critiquing alongside me. To Lara Saguisag, Ebony Harding, Coe Booth, and Daphne Benedis-Grab for always listening and answering. To Alyssa Eisner Henkin, Jennifer Rees, and David Levithan for the best present a girl could imagine and for encouraging me to take another look. To all of my friends and family who requested copies when *Sellout* was just an idea, I appreciate you all.